BLOOD SECRETS

Nadine McInnis

BLOOD SECRETS

STORIES

BIBLIOASIS

FIRST EDITION

Library and Archives Canada Cataloguing in Publication

McInnis, Nadine, 1957-
        Blood secrets / Nadine McInnis.

Short Stories.
ISBN 978-1-926845-93-7

        I. Title.

PS8575.I54B56 2012   C813'.54   C2012-901708-6

Canada Council for the Arts   Conseil des Arts du Canada   ONTARIO ARTS COUNCIL
CONSEIL DES ARTS DE L'ONTARIO

Canadian Heritage   Patrimoine canadien

Biblioasis acknowledges the ongoing financial support of the Government of Canada through the Canada Council for the Arts, Canadian Heritage, the Canada Book Fund; and the Government of Ontario through the Ontario Arts Council.

Cover Image by Eduardo Gomez

PRINTED AND BOUND IN CANADA

Contents

The Story of Time

O N THE NIGHT SHE MET HIM, one century was becoming another. Joyce was with her husband and daughter on Parliament Hill. Europe had celebrated all through the day, with flamenco dancers in Spain, an explosion of light behind the Eiffel Tower, parades and spectacles so energetic that they came downtown that night, expecting something spectacular to happen as the timeline moved closer.

Joyce could tell by the edginess of the crowd, primed with liquor and shifting in the cold, that she was not the only one irritated by the sombre sound-and-light show called *The Story of Time.* Costumed dancers paraded around the peripheries carrying puppets that were supposed to be cogs in the machinery of a giant clock wheeling freely around them. Bleak modern art was projected onto the Peace Tower as speakers broadcast a collision of twentieth-century sounds: children screaming, air raid sirens and industrial rackets. She looked to see what effect this was having on her daughter. Ruth's hands in their thick mittens were clamped on either side of her angular face, pulling her skin tight over her fine bones.

"Can we go now? I hate this," Ruth said. And then again, "I hate this."

"You're not kidding. This is what gives art a bad name. All that angst and seriousness," Colin said. "All that bullshit about the *zeitgeist* of the times."

"The great critic speaks," Joyce said, annoyed.

He ignored her testiness, stretched out his arms, ready to wrap them both in his tall embrace, but he held a silver flask open in one hand. Joyce could see him considering which one of them he would hug. It was a split-second decision. She felt a fleeting disappointment when he put his arm around their daughter while reaching to offer the flask to her. Joyce shook her head, shivering at the thought of the small metal O, wet with saliva, unbearably cold in her mouth.

Red and gold spotlights swept over two mountain climbers from the armed forces as they scaled the tower at two minutes to midnight, ascending through an image of the earth taken from space, heading towards the white face of the clock.

"Those poor buggers," Colin said. "To have to be the star attraction in this noise-in-the-dark show. Only in Canada."

"You're the one who wanted your citizenship so badly I had to marry you," Joyce said.

He laughed, not noticing her tone, and said, "You had a few other enticements. Sea to sea to sea. I know them all by now."

"That's what you think." She decided to let it go. "We need to find something worth coming downtown for tonight. After all, how often does the millennium change?"

"Too bloody often, if this is all we have to look forward to." This is the way he talked when he drinks, a little crude, which made Joyce turn her face away from him.

The countdown was projected onto the Peace Tower as the crowd called out the numbers half-heartedly. They called down to seven, then the number on the Peace Tower jumped up to nine again, before skipping to four, which flashed upside down. The voices petered out to confused silence so that the number one hung in the air, and then, without any fanfare at all, the millennium changed. Fireworks started and ended even before the crowd had the chance to shift their attention to the northern sky. The concussion she usually felt in the centre of her chest was muffled by her winter coat.

"Well, that was an experience," Colin said, as the crowd turned with one mind away from the Parliament Buildings towards the few openings in the fence. "I think I'll go home and drown my sorrows in whisky."

"You already have." She glanced over to see if her daughter was listening to them.

"Those terrible sounds, especially the crying children,—they made me think there really had been some sort of terrorist attack," Ruth said. She seemed to be shrugging off her own discomfort now that the broadcast noises had stopped.

SECURITY HAD BEEN TIGHT on the way in. All fifty thousand in the crowd were frisked with metal detectors, but the narrow gaps in the makeshift fence were not sufficient to let fifty thousand out.

Now, no one stands at the exits, not a uniform in sight, yet the fences remain standing. A subtle drift can be felt. Joyce is almost lifted from her feet, an irresistible pressure separating her from Colin and Ruth who are swept away in a different direction. So this is how people are trampled to death, she thinks, as though stating a fact that has nothing to do with her. She is being pushed by a heavy soundless wave, isolating, yet singling her out for obliteration. She can't breathe with the pressure exerted from all sides, like being under black water, trying to come up for air. The stars spin above her, cold salt falling through the dark, salt she can almost taste on her tongue. She feels her feet moving automatically without really bearing her full weight on the ground.

Pressed insistently against someone else, she lowers her eyes to see a man looking away.

He has a vague grimace on his face, is warding her off with his forearm pushed up until she can smell the cloth of his sleeve, dry cleaning fluid and good wool, his hand between their faces. Then he manages to lift it further as though there is something floating in the air above their heads, something elusive, like a feather, and he wants to pluck it out of the darkness. Her chest pushes hard against his chest. She's glad for their winter coats and hopes he is stronger than he looks. He is about her height, his face strong and tense around the jaw, eyes slightly unfocused as though he is lost in thought. His breath, thickened by the cold, moves unpleasantly along her cheek with a faint fresh smell of mint. She is off balance with her attempts to lean away from him, she knows she will be lost without him to push against. Hip to hip, feet moving in a kind of desperate dance, weight about equal, they remain upright like two delicately balanced cards.

"I'm not doing this on purpose," Joyce says.

"I know. I'm not doing it either." He looks at her directly for the first time.

"My arm," he says. "I can't hold it up any longer." And his arm drifts down and rests lightly across her shoulder. She curls in closer, not being able to tell if it is her will or something else pushing her into this familiarity. A sudden lurch travels through the crowd and then her nose is in his neck, a cool silver smell. He isn't wearing a hat and she can smell the shampoo from his hair.

Now, the gap in the fence is just ahead and there is a renewed pressure, an urgency pushing painfully towards that point of entry and exit. Her arm moves up to steady her and then it floats around his neck, and she feels his arm, surprisingly strong around the small of her back, holding her upright. Bodies press in all around, the smell of alcohol cloying just over their heads. It feels impossible to get a clean breath.

"Almost there," he tells her and for the first time, smiles more generously than she would have expected from his serious, private face. The temporary gatepost opening out to Wellington Street is circled with phosphorescent tape. She focuses, counting the distance to keep herself calm: three metres, then two, finally one, then a push, a collective groan from the crowd, the most dangerous moment. Pushed so hard, she can't fill her lungs. Their bodies fly apart, but they are propelled in the same direction. He is still watching her as she takes a deep breath.

"I usually don't do that on the first date," she tells him, but he doesn't laugh. Now people are hurtling past, near misses, like dark stars. She tries to catch sight of Colin and Ruth, but they were separated such a long way back.

"Did you lose someone?" he asks.

"My husband and daughter."

He looks at his feet then as though this is a rebuke, and she notes that he is wearing black dress shoes.

"Aren't your feet cold?"

"I hadn't planned this. I just finished work." He says this hurriedly, and she can see that he is a shy man.

"Was *The Story of Time* worth risking your life for?"

He laughs. A surprise. She has already written him off. "It was a bit bleak. Maybe there are troubled times ahead," he says.

"Maybe," and she turns away.

"I can help you," he says. "If you want."

A wave of distaste washes through her. It occurs to her that he might pull a pamphlet from his pocket. *The Watchtower,* or some cranked-out basement mimeograph. She can see the bare arm plunging up and down in bad light. Pockets stuffed full, smeared promises of damnation and catastrophe, fire, ice, floods. He has the shoes for something like that. And the clean-cut hair of a fanatic.

"I'll help you find them."

"But you don't know what they look like," she says, relieved that this is all he means. "Besides, I'll meet them at home."

They start to move for the first time since they are free of the gate. Her legs are a bit shaky. But she doesn't have very far to go to reach the bus stop on Slater Street. She, Colin and Ruth had taken a bus downtown, with crowds of young people drinking and laughing, wearing long evening dresses under their winter jackets, no hats or mitts. But by the time she inches down through the crowd to where the buses are running, she can see that getting home will mean throwing herself back into that tangled mass of humanity. The crowd is now a little drunker, a little meaner, and more impatient than they were on the Hill.

"I don't think I can face that now," she says. Her legs have stopped shaking, but feel heavy and jelled, as though her bones were filled with mercury. She has never been good with crowds.

All around, people are sweeping them along, still blowing their noisemakers. A few revelers crack light sticks, releasing an eerie green glow that soon grows faint. Some are writing on the air with sparklers. Lovely, fiery hieroglyphs, tantalizing secrets fading into darkness. She is trying to read these messages lit in the air when a young man stumbles into her path. Then she is down too, and as she falls, her brow explodes, a crystal glassy sound, followed by a warm flood down the side of her face. A woman reaches to lift her, crying out, "Are you all right? You're bleeding."

The woman is holding an empty champagne glass in one hand as though she has thrown the drink in Joyce's face. There is a kind of hot sparkling pain, not cold like champagne. But there is very little discomfort after that initial flash. The woman drops the stem of a broken glass from her other hand and it shatters like an icicle on the hard street. Joyce waves her off, confused. Was the woman carrying one glass or two? Is she injured or not? Is it champagne or blood running down her face?

Then he is beside her, gently pressing a folded scarf to her forehead. She leans hard against his hand to stop the bleeding and feels sudden sharp pain.

"Don't press. There could be glass," he says and steps several feet away, bent down. She's dizzy without his support. He walks back, slowly removes her hand and then presses softly packed snow against the cut.

"Lucky for you, my store is just down here," he says, leading her by the arm. Everything is a bit skewed, as she has one eye closed. Soon the snow is melting down her face like tears. Pink bloody tears. She's off balance, but he keeps her moving more or less in a straight line. The crowd parts to let them through.

"And you just happen to be a doctor," she says, once she sees the store with her one open eye. A large modern drugstore lit up with a neon elongated blue cross. When he doesn't answer, she adds, "That cross is just like something from the Crusades."

"Neon was one of the great inventions of the twentieth century," he says. They are speaking in riddles and she doesn't know if she is meant to laugh.

"Along with management theory applied to genocide, light pollution and frogs with four legs." Then she does laugh. She doesn't know where this list has come from. Some unknown part of her is thinking fast.

He's silent again. They can't seem to find any reliable rhythm to their conversation.

She realizes that she's recently been in this store. Just a few blocks from here, at the Museum of Nature, she's been doing life studies of birds for a children's book she is illustrating. On a break, she has bought lipstick here, a fiery red she carries in her purse.

He searching for keys from inside his coat, zipped away in a pocket that she has never seen any other man use.

"I'm not a doctor. I'm a pharmacist. I have bandages, ointment, anesthetic."

"Imagine that." Pain makes her sarcastic. She can't tell if she really means to insult him or if it's just a way of drawing him out. He takes his time before answering.

"If you'd rather not," he says, turning to look at her, waiting for her to set the tone for what remains of their encounter. She sees that he is willing to make her wait as long as it takes for her to make up her mind.

"Thank you. I would rather not leave a trail of blood behind me."

He turns then, opens the door and steps inside the dim large room. He punches codes and flips one switch. A light comes on far back in the store where the drugs are stored on shelves in large plastic jars. But it is dark. He notices her discomfort.

"And I'd rather not let the world know that we're here."

But she doesn't find this reassuring. She looks down at her flat practical boots, now leaving a puddle on the grey gleam of his floor. He tries again.

"It seems every hour of the night, people remember things they forgot."

And she laughs. "He has the cure for Alzheimer's as well!"

He grins. She starts to plot to win the next smile, so generous and unexpected they seem.

"Can you make your way back in the dark?"

"This is everyone's fantasy," she tells him, and can immediately feel her face grow hot, but he is walking ahead of her and doesn't notice.

In the gentlest possible way he removes splinters of glass with tweezers he's wiped with rubbing alcohol, cleans the cut with wet gauze. He is left-handed and his wedding ring close to her face comes in and out of focus. The bleeding has stopped.

"I can try every perfume, open every box of chocolates and eat just one," she adds.

He dabs slippery ointment with his finger, a sharp and almost sweaty smell, surprisingly warm after the cool cloth. There are long spaces of silence between them.

"They don't break in here for the chocolate. You have innocent fantasies," he says, letting all the meanings hang in the charged air between them.

He leans forward suddenly and kisses her. There is a strange familiarity in the gentle exploration of his tongue. During the kiss she has the sense that she has been here before, and will be here again.

She also has the sense that she is here, with this still-nameless man, and elsewhere at the same time. She is here with him and yet she is already in her future, at the Museum of Nature, utterly unable to concentrate on the indigo buntings frozen in a facsimile of flight in the diorama of a still northern forest. It will be that kind of a courtship, if courtship is even a word that can describe what they have embarked upon. The first time they meet in daylight, they will walk to the museum. They won't be interested in the static wings of the birds with their innocent voices piped through speakers above their heads. Verisimilitude if they keep their eyes closed: the wind and calls of a gannet colony high on a cliff, the gentle surroundings of an early morning in a boreal forest. All gone when they open their eyes.

§

THE KISS SEEMS TO SET something free in him, and his formality vanishes. He grows animated, moving quickly while talking, a compact man with the precise grace of a dancer. He gives her a tour of the more personal side of his pharmacy: tells her about each of the antique medicine bottles he has collected and placed on locked glass shelves near the cash. He turns on a light set behind the bottles in such a way that the cobalt blue or amber or deep brown of the glass glows wet and luminous as though each bottle hasn't yet hardened after being fired and shaped. Then he leads her to a back room, opens the door, and she wonders what he might unleash. The light is intense as she steps through the door.

"Welcome to my pharmaceutical garden, or my physic garden, as they used to be called," he says. Under the grow lights are shelves of herbs and flowering plants, the damp floor is concrete, but there is a sitting area with a plush red couch, a carefully made-up single bed and a bathroom off to the side.

"Do you live here?" she asks, incredulous.

"It's a place to recharge, a place to dream," he says.

"What else do you get up to in here? I suppose many of these plants are intoxicants."

"Some, but just as many cure and clear the head. This is fever-few, good for old-style melancholia."

"How is this different from new-style melancholia?" she says.

He doesn't answer, so absorbed is he in his plants. She's drawn to the lush purple of violets with leaves as dewy and heart-shaped as springtime.

"Not your grandmother's African violets," she says.

"No, those are from Ireland. In the Middle Ages the petals were tied to the forehead to cure insomnia," he says. "And this is evening primrose. You must know what this is for."

"Oh, yes," she says. "It makes women raging with hormones as docile as lambs."

"Only if picked at certain times. Such as when the moon is full, or close to the solstice."

"Like now. It's powerful now?"

"Yes, I guess so," he says before moving on to other plants. She is mostly quiet then, listening attentively and instinctively, as she would after dark in a forest, her senses heightened. The stone pestle she picks up and holds in her hands quickly grows warm, like heavy flesh.

His hand touches hers and it's as warm as the stone she holds. He says, "That once belonged to an apothecary. It was dug up from an ancient garbage dump several metres down from the surface of the earth we live on at this moment."

"Strange," she says. "To look around at everything and think of that." And she shivers, thinking of the hollow sound of her own voice on the answering machine when she called home to see if anyone was there.

BEFORE THEY LEAVE the pharmacy, he carefully tears a mint leaf, serrated and emerald, from a plant on the counter and she automatically opens her mouth although he hasn't told her what to do. But it's the right thing. He places the leaf on her tongue. She thinks of the coca leaves that Aztecs used to place on their tongues for spiritual journeys.

As he's locking the door, she feels time speeding up. Everything has collided so quickly, she's disoriented, as though her family is a distant memory. Even though she doesn't know if she will ever see this man again.

ONE THING FOLLOWED ANOTHER until all that followed eventually became part of her past. She often wondered at what point her life became inevitable. If he hadn't kissed her, and she hadn't responded with a welcoming curiosity, would the memory of him have been dim, a memory of a kindness rather than of a man? Could even that kiss have been remembered as just another New Year's kiss, intemperate, drunken and easily disregarded in daylight?

He drove her home that night in his elegant car with heated seats, the streets still full of drunken people. On her tongue, the mint leaf tingled. Yet it felt strange to bid him good night and turn towards the door of her apartment building.

She watched for Ruth and Colin from the frigid screened-in balcony of their second-floor apartment, where year by year they could feel gravity pulling them towards the enveloping maple pressed against the screen. She had carefully walked up the driveway, stepping into their earlier footprints in new snow when she returned, a superstition left over from childhood, so that it looked as though no one had come home yet. She was already a ghost in her own life.

When her family stamped off the snow in the hallway and opened the door, she was waiting to greet them. As it happened, they had waited at the bus stop for her, retraced their steps several times to look for her, growing more and more worried. Her husband was prepared to call the police, and was obviously surprised to find her home. Their faces were the faces of ones loved long ago, and she was overjoyed to see them again.

Ruth gave her hug, telling her, "I thought you were gone, like those people who spontaneously combust."

The three of them laughed at this, and how appropriate it would be for something as dramatic as that to happen on the night the millennium changed.

Soon after, she lay beneath Colin, as he slowly peeled back the bandage on her brow.

"Admit it," he said. "You were out carousing and brawling."

"You should see the other guy."

"Oh, my fierce, fierce woman." And he kissed the cut above her eye, now just a thin red line.

She slept, her knee against Colin's thigh, her breast molded against his smooth back. She dreamt they were standing face to face. Her groin to his groin, she held a snake in her hand, weaving it around their waists. But the man she dreamt of was not her husband. The man in her dream was still a stranger, although soon she would be standing on a busy street corner with him and saying his name, telling him she loved him.

"The air temperature is -8, the sun will set at 4:47 P.M. And I love ... " and she would say his name, Ferrall, a strange name that once belonged to his mother as her maiden name. It was a name that she loved for its uniqueness, not diminished even when it grew quickly familiar.

"These are facts," she would say, knowing that he liked facts, the predictability of chemistry, the novel logic of an absurd explanation. Even as she said it, she knew it wasn't true, but she said it anyway, as though correlation of facts with willfulness made her less culpable. And she suspected even then that she would only know him for a short time. He would prove to be a timid man—so eager to elicit response in her, so uneasy once he had succeeded. His eyes were not filled with kindness, as she had first thought, but merely distance, always focused elsewhere.

SOON AFTER, SHE WALKED the four blocks from the museum to the pharmacy to return his washed scarf. The holiday season was finally over and the store was busy as people recalled their daily needs and aggravations. She lined up behind women who talked to him about birth control, blood thinners, anti-inflammatory drugs and skin creams. But ills and deficiencies had nothing to do with her.

When it was her turn, she said, "You know all our secrets," and was shocked that he didn't seem to recognize her with her washed hair loose around her collar, her fearless red mouth. He smiled with recognition once she placed his folded scarf on the counter.

"Only the secrets of the body," he said.

"Are there any other kind?" she asked.

He left the store to the care of others and they walked through windy streets cut off from the sun by high office towers. She knew no one here, her neighbourhood being the ramshackle apartments of other artists and carpenters in an older residential area. They entered a frozen park where blocks of ice, tantalizingly transparent but indecipherable, had been delivered in preparation for the carvers to begin their sculptures for winter carnival.

"I want to see your drawings," he said and cleared snow off a bench, his black gloved hand sifting through insubstantial glitter.

He turned each page of her pad slowly. When he came to the sand hill cranes dancing, hopping with huge muscular wings outspread, he laughed.

"Very whimsical."

"They're for a children's book about the family behaviour of birds. Although this dance isn't something you would do in front of the young ones." She felt she was apologizing, but he looked at her with frank curiosity and she started to relax. "I use the birds at the museum for models."

"I haven't been there for years."

"You've raised children?" she asked. Her hands were getting cold and she put her gloves back on, not looking at him when he answered, "I still do," without offering anything more.

They walked along Metcalfe Street to the museum, a stone castle guarded by carved mastodons. At the top of the sweeping marble stairway they watched the giant pterodactyls frozen in flight, circling, with salmon in their beaks. Their tour was almost wordless, moving quickly through time, from the formation of the earth's crust to the fossil record of tropical ferns found in northern Canada. They stood before the bird dioramas, each parallel reality so believable because the taped sounds were so immediate—fog shrouding the windy cliffs in one, sunshine in a winter forest in another. Joyce felt as though she was on display, inhabiting her own discordant diorama, the climate-controlled environment of the museum all wrong for her racing heart.

They didn't go near the floor that had been Ruth's favourite when she was younger, the room tucked away on the top where the living were housed among the dead. In large aquariums, banana slugs left their slow trails of slime across broad green leaves. Ruth would dash from that aquarium to the next one, putting her small hands against the glass that contained a filthy kitchen sink where cockroaches furtively dashed from rusted tin can to the underside of a crusted plate. These reminders of what could live beneath the surface of the world she recognized interested her far more than dinosaur bones.

OVER THE YEARS, there would be attempts to overcome the distance between Joyce and Ruth, on both their parts. Before Ruth had her own family, when it still might matter to her to set things right with her own mother, they had spent a weekend together at a spa in rural Quebec in the dead of winter. There were few people registered. Nobody spoke their language so they were quite alone with each other, at first laughing and joking about the ridiculously relaxed bodies sleeping in bathrobes all over the public spaces—women with sagging chests lying inert on sofas in the lobby, snoring beside the roaring fireplace. The faux-peaceful music of birdsong piped throughout the treatment rooms gave them both fits of giggles whenever they looked at each other.

Joyce was delighted with how easy this felt, and hoped that trouble was all behind them. She thought that now she would be free to talk about the past. They happened to be there on Valentine's Day, an occasion that didn't mean much to either of them. Joyce had not remarried; Ruth dated rarely and never sustained a relationship long enough for Joyce to learn a young man's name. This trip away would be a way of celebrating themselves. Joyce scheduled facials for the two of them. They giggled together as the attendant brushed a cold slimy substance on their faces.

"Yuck. Snail slime," Ruth said.

"Slug spittle," Joyce answered.

"Frog spawn," Ruth said.

They were laughing so hard, so infectiously, that the attendant had to wait, brush in hand for them to calm down. A drop of clear thick fluid dropped from the bristles onto Joyce's lap.

"I hope you're using protection, Mom," Ruth said, starting a new gale of laughter. Joyce was a little shocked, but not as shocked as she was the day before when she saw her daughter's body on the table next to hers, naked, before the layers of algae were wrapped around her. It was a woman's body, ready for all that nature expected of it, with full tipped-up breasts and a delicate concave belly waiting to be filled. But her daughter's body was marked too. With faint silver scars along it. Some of these scars Joyce had known about, from the piercings she got through that winter of 2000, before Joyce left home. The rest were fine cut marks on the softest parts of her flesh.

When the attendant left the room, telling them to keep still for "une demi-heure," Joyce thought that Ruth's comment had given her the opening to talk about that time.

"Do you remember the winter you were sick? When you got all the piercings and that horrible infection? I was going through something difficult too. Something I couldn't explain to you at the time."

She took Ruth's silence to mean that she was ready to listen, so she told about her own distraction, her own craziness that winter. It was her attempt to finally bring those two conflicting worlds together, although she couldn't say his name to her daughter, even now. She hoped she didn't sound self-centred, even though she knew that's what she had been then.

"You think I didn't know?" Ruth said.

"You knew?"

"I didn't want to know. Dad might have been blind, but I wasn't. Don't tell me any more. It makes me mad to think about how careless you were, how little you cared really."

Joyce was shocked.

"I cared," she said.

She hoped Ruth heard her regret, but the conversation seemed to be over. The silence between them was hardening like a carapace.

THAT WINTER WHEN EVERYTHING blew apart, there had been a disappointment for Ruth—a relationship that didn't survive. That much, Joyce had known. Later in the winter, she had seen her daughter standing under the street light outside their second-storey apartment with the shadowy figure of a boy. Snow swirled around them and the shape of the thick light made it look as though the storm raged around them alone. They were obviously arguing. Ruth bent forward slightly from the hips, her face pointed upwards so that she took the snow and wind full force. Now and then she raised her arms emphatically. Joyce didn't pay much attention to the young man, apart from noticing his height and the way he was half-turned away from her daughter, edging out from under the streetlight's pale storm. Then he would step back into the centre, back into the disagreement they were having. It was a painful dance, with her daughter assuming the lead.

At the time, Joyce had been fascinated by her daughter's passion. She felt a thrilling kinship with her, completely different from the protective bond she had felt up to then. Alert to any other woman's sexuality, she hadn't expected this new keening awareness would be directed at her own daughter. That winter, she imagined a time when the two of them would talk about their relationships and about the secret that was distracting her from her life.

She hadn't thought of Ruth's pain. But perhaps Ruth had been trying to reawaken the maternal in her because soon after, she stopped washing, and soon after that, stopped eating. Colin was hectoring in his determination to get Ruth to eat, until Joyce, late in their bedroom one night, said, "Leave her be. She's a teenager."

"Leave her to waste away? Leave her to die? Like you do?"

"Don't be so melodramatic."

"Where are you? Where are you living? Not with us, I'll tell you that," he said.

Joyce didn't answer. He was too close to the truth for her to risk even looking into his face.

"Maybe it's time you thought about coming home," he said.

She couldn't, and didn't know then that she would never find her way back home. Her daughter had transformed into this gaunt damaged stranger. She wanted to avoid her. The rank desperate smell of her, the lids that only appeared half-opened over enormous grey irises filled her with restlessness. She didn't want to be like this feral female she was living with, simmering with self-destructiveness. There was a sexual, heavy-hooded look to her daughter's eyes that made Joyce feel both repulsed and resentful.

Then came the piercings, through the eyebrow, fish hooks in a line along her ear, a bolt through the back of her neck. Then a gold ring almost as wide as a wedding ring through her lower lip.

"How is anyone supposed to kiss her?" Joyce said to Colin.

"I think that's the point," he said, without accusing her further.

Soon, she heard her daughter moaning with pain in her sleep and went in one night when she couldn't bear the distance between them. She put her hand on Ruth's forehead and found her drenched with fever, her mouth angry red. Her thin body had not been strong enough to heal the wound of the last piercing and had become infected.

Joyce went to his pharmacy for antibiotics. Later she wondered if she had been trying to sabotage the affair by making him fill the prescription, forcing him to see how much damage had been done. She had talked to him about Ruth, wanting to draw him into the next level of intimacy.

But as she stood in line, she watched him gently cajole another woman who had a fur collar that seemed to bristle and crackle with energy under the florescent lights. She saw him pluck a mint leaf from the plant he kept under grow lights on the counter. The woman opened her mouth and he placed the leaf on her tongue. She could hear the woman's laugh and his eyes were still bright when she reached the counter with her piece of paper, so flimsy and dead compared to the mint leaf. She, too, had often felt the tingling in her mouth that winter, the sensation lasting until she got home. It was a secret she carried after all the other traces of him were carefully washed away in the shower.

Just seeing that gesture, a replica of that private interchange that, between them, had seemed almost sacred, started to turn her away from him. He seemed to know that a change was taking place. He was efficient with her, professionally deferential as he answered her questions about the strength of the antibiotic, and even more so when she filled the first prescription for antidepressants for her daughter soon afterwards. Another prescription followed by another as Ruth sickened and reeled through a frightening array of side effects: tremors, nausea, nightmares as terrifying as the first nightmares of her early childhood. There was dizziness and muscle twitches and blinding headaches until Ruth cried, "You're poisoning me. Get away from me." The only solution was for Joyce to take her at her word and leave.

In a makeshift apartment, she lay awake far into the night and remembered the moment when any future was ahead—her life with Colin and Ruth, not yet laid down and lost, not yet buried under yards of discarded debris like a medieval village known only by layers of garbage metres below the surface.

"IT'S STOPPED HURTING," she says to the stranger who is tapping gently at the bandage above her eye, making sure it will stay in place. She can see the slanted face of his silver watch, the minute hand already halfway into the first hour of a new millennium. And beyond his watch, she looks down the dark tunnel of his cuff at the hairless underside of his wrist.

"You're a shaman. I'm perfectly healed."

She can't help the flirtatious tone of her voice. He scares her. Being here scares her. His smell is so unfamiliar, yet strangely inevitable.

"Maybe you're a quick healer," he says. "But you may have a scar. The skin is thin on the forehead."

"Oh, no," she answers. "I never scar."

"Never?" he challenges.

"I am an athlete when it comes to pain."

He laughs.

"And why is that?" he says.

"Because I'm an artist."

"So, you are an artist," he states. "And you like pain."

"I don't like pain. I don't go looking for it, but I tolerate it well enough. And I've gotten this far without any scars at all," she says, knowing that although she may never see him after this strange new hour of a new millennium, this is a challenge. She's aware of the white expanse of her winter skin. She sees him considering what she has told him.

"Everyone has a scar somewhere."

"Well, maybe one. See these little teeth marks under my lip?" She pulls her lip up with her teeth as he leans in closer. "I was jumping on my bed when I was four years old and I jumped too high. My teeth went right through when I landed on the floor. But I don't remember it happening at all." She pauses, watching him smile at her.

"It's a wonderful quality. That forgetfulness," he said.

"So you see, I won't scar. I promise," she says, putting one hand over her heart. This gesture is the turning point, she will recognize years later. Feeling her heart beating under her hand is the moment when a strange little incident takes on its own momentum. Even then, she knows she is a fool. But looking around her, she also feels an irresistible need to go with the momentum, to take a chance on what fate has cast onto her path.

She fixes this moment in her memory, certain that now that she is aware of her own power, it will always belong to her. She is still almost young, sitting among the Orbis backrests shrouded in plastic, next to a vat of canes and a carrel display of reading glasses and chains. All around them are reminders of decrepitude, deterioration, but she feels full of energy. The edges of everything in the drugstore are backlit with a cool metallic light, dim yet potent. Crowds of strangers still stream past the dark windows, unable to see in.

Heart of Blue, Glowing

J OYCE ALWAYS CAME HOME from the hospice with a list of names in her pocket, even though she had found that names didn't matter much there. From week to week, the names changed, as they were expected to, even though the room numbers, one to eight, stayed the same. Old-fashioned names, ready to come into popular circulation again: Dorothy, Grace, Daniel, Sarah, Isaiah, Daisy, Joe, shifting from generation to generation as if carried on the wind.

Today two candles remained lit by the nurses' station, as they were for 24 hours after a death, and two new patients had already arrived by ambulance. The flames flickered each time someone passed by, two little hearts beating from all the activity of the two nurses and two volunteers on duty. The settling-in period was always a busy one for volunteers who had more time for listening than the nurses. And the families were usually distraught.

Joyce heard a commotion even before she finished writing down names.

"Joyce, can you check in on Isaiah and his family?" the nurse said.

"Sure," she called back, although she didn't yet know which room held Isaiah. She followed the sound.

She stepped around the screen in room five. Three women were filling up the room, all tall, all in their thirties. They seemed to be having an argument about art.

"Washed out faux-impressionism. You can't expect him to look at that all day," one of the women said. She was straight-backed and pierced with silver through her eyebrow, and carried herself with the upward tilt to her jaw of a woman who was used to being looked at. Her hands braced the frame of a painting, ready to lift it off the wall.

"Give it a rest, George. He's not here on a fellowship. Do you think he cares?" The woman who said this was sitting at the end of his bed. She held herself with the same erect carriage but was dressed in a navy skirt and pale blue sweater.

"He cares! His life is art," George said. Without acknowledging Joyce, she passed the painting of lily pads into her hands.

"This is not the time," the third woman said. She was more tentative than her sisters, gazing down at the small figure in the bed.

Joyce looked at the man too, who seemed to be sleeping. He was thin, probably exhausted from the transition from hospital to this room where he would soon die. He was probably eating very little at this stage. His skin was translucent, smoky-coloured, beautiful, like old polished wood. The calm sculptural quality of him was reinforced by the static of conflict in the room.

"He wouldn't want this," George insisted.

"How do you know what he wants? Where have you been all year?"

She ignored this, flicking her hand at the painting Joyce was now holding in her hands. This transfer had taken place without Joyce quite noticing how. Not wanting to make any move that would seem to be taking sides, Joyce stood by quietly. "How can you stand to watch people die?" a friend had asked her. But she felt that what she did here was watch people live, a vivid strange time in their lives, full of dreams and memories, the undercurrents of their family intensifying, time breaking down between past and present. Often the families were harder to watch than the patient, maybe because there would not be any foreseeable relief.

George's voice brought her back. "Not visual pablum. I can tell you that. He's an artist."

"Right now, he's a sick man," the woman sitting on the bed said. "What he needs is for us to get along. At this late date."

"He should have his own paintings around him. Representational art is dead."

"Fine choice of words."

Joyce thought the moment had come to say something.

"I wondered if there is anything I can do for you or your father to help settle in?" She hoped she had guessed correctly at the family relationship.

"You're doing it," George said. "You're going to carry that awful painting right out of the room."

One of the other women hissed at her, "Do you have to be so rude? My God."

"What's your name?" George said, and Joyce reluctantly told her, not wanting to be drawn in to the personal dynamic between the women.

"Joyce," George said as though she had known her for years. "You tell me. Is this painting a cliché or what?"

"It's a matter of taste," Joyce replied. "Some people might find the colours soothing." She noticed the tension in her voice, as though she was defending her own paintings. What would George have to say about her watercolour hung in the hallway—indigo buntings against fresh snow. Joyce had donated it before she decided to become a volunteer.

"And some people might be put to sleep," George retorted, and laughed. "Just like a dog."

"I can't stand it. Stop it. Just, stop it," the quiet one said.

Joyce moved closer to one of the paintings on the wall, and then she understood what the problem was with George. She could smell liquor and desperation, stale sweat, contradicting her haughty authority.

LAST WINTER, she had first come to this hospice with Ferrall, who used to personally deliver medications from his pharmacy on Friday nights when his drivers were off duty. At the time, she saw this as a sign of his sensitivity, a little act of chivalry that helped to justify how she was deceiving her husband. But once he had gone through the door and left her alone for what often turned into a long time, she felt closed out of his life, and increasingly closed off from her own family.

She sat in his car in the parking lot, waiting as the car grew colder and colder and the windows steamed over from her breath. She cleared the glass from time to time and water with the consistency of tears gathered and rolled slowly down, distorting the lights from the low building blocking out the frozen river that she knew was there at the end of the garden. He had forgotten to leave her the keys so she could warm up and she felt that first flare of irritation. Where was he? But she wouldn't have thought of entering the hospice, which was part of his other life, any more than she could imagine him walking through her front door at home.

Once she saw a patient in a wheelchair, swaddled in a too-large jacket and a handmade quilt, smoking at a summer patio table. Joyce hadn't wanted to look too closely at the fragile form. In the pit of her stomach she felt a kick, and thought of Ruth. Her daughter had become dangerously thin last winter, before Joyce left home. Ruth would sit in the living room wrapped in her old baby blanket, with her dark-circled eyes and pointy bones, staring into space. Planting herself in the centre of the household, wanting to make sure her mother noticed.

Joyce couldn't believe a whole year had passed and so much had changed. Colin and Ruth went on without her, and Ruth's health returned. At the time, she wouldn't have been able to admit it, but in the months since living on her own she had come to realize that she had closed herself off from Ruth for much longer than the year she had been gone. She had chosen her own body's needs over her daughter's and she would pay for this for the rest of her life. In the meantime, she was caught in this in-between world, not with them, but not yet anywhere else.

Ferrall was gone from her life too, sooner than she would have thought, and she found herself walking by the hospice fairly often without understanding why. She donated a painting and soon after made an appointment to inquire about volunteering.

The nurse who had interviewed her asked, "Why do you want to do this?"

Joyce didn't know consciously what to say but knew that she must be absolutely honest.

"Because I've lost people I love. And it doesn't make any sense to me at all."

She was surprised at her answer, hadn't thought of it before now.

"Your parents?"

"In a way," Joyce said, hearing the avoidance in her own voice.

"I have a difficult relationship with my mother. It's going to be very hard for me when her time comes." Once again, Joyce was surprised by how true this was.

"How will this help?" the nurse asked.

"I will learn what I can give and how. At least the process of dying will be familiar."

"Is your father alive?" The nurse asked.

"Yes, but I'm not in touch with him."

The nurse waited.

"My parents divorced many years ago."

"What about you? Do you have a family?"

"I'm separated."

"Children?"

"One, a daughter who is seventeen now. She lives with her father."

"So you're still actively mothering."

She wondered about this phrase, whether she was still mothering. Or was she actively absent the way her own mother had been?

The nurse seemed to pick up on her thoughts and asked, "Is your separation recent?"

"Not too recent," she answered. Again, the nurse waited.

"But unexpected. I never thought I would be on my own at this stage in my life."

"Many people who find themselves here as patients feel the same way," she said. "Would you say that you're still grieving?"

"Probably. I'm a little disoriented. I guess I need to learn how to let go, and also how to live in a different way."

She was sure that she would be rejected on the basis of what she had said, that her reasons were too tainted with personal failure. But the nurse was saying that she admired the painting Joyce had donated months before and was glad to meet the person who had created it. Then they talked about aloneness and human connection and aging.

Finally, the nurse said, "Your reasons are not so uncommon. Helping people through the last stage of life can be a spiritual experience for everyone. But, you'll see the opposite too. Family dynamics become exaggerated. If something strikes too close to home, you'll have to recognize that and take care of yourself. You won't be a help to anyone if you're wrestling with your own ghosts."

So she took a course, every Wednesday night for three months, conscientiously reading from the book list, *Final Gifts, What Dying People Want*, and still knew nothing. But she did learn the proper way to lift and bathe someone too weak to hold themselves up, how water can be thickened for people who have trouble swallowing, that the best she could do for someone was attentive listening, with little of her own life offered in return. She had taken the lessons to heart. She had tried to empty herself of desire. She tried to take people exactly as they were, without judgment or expectations. And the way they accepted her presence, without judgment, seemed the greatest gift. Before long, she gave up her name, feeling no need to introduce herself when she entered someone's room. Only her humanness was relevant.

It was a coincidence that she ended up working on Friday nights. The weekend shifts were harder to fill, and being an artist who worked on her own time, she could fit in anywhere without difficulty. She saw Ferrall from a distance a couple of times. He just waved casually. Every time she saw him, he was leaning against the counter talking to the receptionist. Often he would still be there the next time she walked down the corridor to escort a visitor back to a room or retrieve a drug delivery. It was like they had never known each other.

Those cold nights she had waited for him in the car, she had assumed that he was being consulted about medications. She used to imagine him with his hand on someone's head, just as he had ministered to her on the night she met him. It was a surprise to realize that he'd probably forgotten about her waiting in his car outside.

§

WHEN SHE NEXT ENTERED Isaiah's room, she was almost assaulted by the paintings on the walls. Instead of the usual floral watercolours, the walls gave the impression of leaning, almost toppling, from the weight of huge canvases hung around the bed. They were fiercely abstract, crackling scarlet beneath bands of black, harsh whites and queasy yellows like the colour of the sky before thunderstorms. She recognized the style, should have known him from his name. The paintings were violently passionate and masculine.

Isaiah was lying on his side, with a pillow propping him and was absolutely still so she couldn't tell if he was awake until she walked around his bed. He smiled vaguely when she said hello. She had been briefed about the ongoing arguments between his three grown daughters, all within two years of age, all with different mothers. George was the youngest and was responsible for mounting his paintings on the walls. She had lived the longest with their father growing up, even if it only amounted to a year or two more than Savannah, who worked for the government. Jill, the silent sister, hadn't lived with him at all. The three sisters were in the family lounge with the door closed. They had been disturbing the other patients.

She looked around the room once Isaiah had acknowledged her presence and said, "Your paintings are powerful. So full of energy." She didn't tell him that she had seen them before at the gallery.

He just gazed at her without responding. His irises were brown, or maybe hazel, darkened with countless specks of dark brown, giving his eyes an eerie cognition.

"I brought you a glass of juice," she said, and he nodded and gestured for her to sit.

"Would you like some wine? Just wait a minute and I'll get you a glass," he said so softly she had to lean forward. He was trying to lift his head off the pillow.

"Thank you. But I'm fine," she said, drawn in by his hospitable ways.

She pulled her chair closer to the bed and angled the straw into his mouth. His big hand came up and touched her hand as she held the glass. He concentrated and it took a minute before she saw that fluid had lifted as far as his lips. His skin was dry and almost scorchingly hot. She was moved by the way heat raged in the bodies of many at the end of life, as though the people inside were in a hurry to spend it all, burn it all, like the fiery end of chlorophyll. After a few minutes, he ran out of strength and let the straw fall.

They sat then, looking at each other, candidly.

"I admire these paintings. They are yours, aren't they?" And she looked behind her to see what he saw from his position in the bed. Once again, she almost gasped at the force of the painting hung there, sharp grey glinting through the bruised blue as though metal had been embedded in the canvas.

"What's this painting called? Do you name your paintings, or give them numbers, like so many abstract painters do? Like Study in Blue, No. 2."

Once again he ignored what she had said and continued to look at her. She considered telling him that she painted as well, but before she said anything, the importance of this slipped away. His daughters had been trying to keep him connected to what had most strongly identified him in life, and she would be doing the same.

She held his gaze, knowing that his eyes were probably the least changed. She didn't look at the bony arms or shrunken shoulders although she wanted to glance down at his hands, so beautiful and precise and generous in size were they now that their bone structure was revealed.

He said something to her that she couldn't catch. His voice was low and loose, as though he was having a chuckle under his breath.

"I'm sorry. I missed that," she said.

He pointed to a stack of *National Geographic* magazines on his side table and said, "At the bottom. He's at the bottom."

She rifled through and he made a sound when she found the torn page beneath the stack. It was a photograph of a terrier sitting on a freshly mowed lawn, looking up at the camera with bright eyes and an eager dog's smile. The white fur on the dog's chest was springy, almost electrified with brushing.

"That's a good boy," he said, and chuckled. "He's a good dog."

"Did you have a dog like this one?" She knew it couldn't be a photo of his own dog because of the jagged edge where it had been ripped out of a magazine.

"He's not mine." He paused, suddenly sad, gazing at the photo she had smoothed on his tray. He pulled the tray closer. She waited because she could tell he had more to say.

"Do you think you could get a frame?" He said this softly, almost under his breath.

"You want to frame this picture?" she asked.

"I asked the girls, but they do what they want." This he said with some bitterness. "Could you bring me a frame? Just a cheap one. I don't care."

"I'll mention it to your daughters."

"Don't bother. They do what they want. Go where they want. They won't find the time. And he's such a good dog. Look at him."

"I can see that."

"The happiest boy in the world," he said, closing his eyes and resting for a minute.

The women came back into the room then. The quiet one, Jill, had clearly been crying. Joyce got up to leave, but George was blocking her way.

"There's that damn dog again," she said. "Dad, do you hear me? Look at the great paintings you've made. Forget the dog."

"He's a good dog," Isaiah said, opening his eyes and glaring at his daughter with more energy than Joyce would have thought he had.

"I told you. I told you, George. Let him have it if he wants it," Jill said.

"If you hadn't brought the magazines in the first place, his mind wouldn't be filled with sentimental trash."

Joyce couldn't leave gracefully. She would have to call attention to herself to clear a path between the sisters.

"Enough," Savannah said to her sisters who were still bickering. "Can't we have some dignity here? This person wants to leave." She gestured towards Joyce.

"She said she'd bring me a frame," Isaiah said.

"Is that true?" George said, ready to turn her anger on Joyce.

"Why don't we talk about it outside," Joyce said. But George wasn't prepared to leave the room to her two sisters.

"Oh, I don't care anymore. Frame whatever you want."

Even from the hall, Joyce could still hear the sisters' voices, kept low now, but clearly irritated and bristling against each other. She wondered about the women missing from the vigil: the mothers who had all been intimate with this man, who had probably loved this man, and had given birth to these women who couldn't stand to be in the same room.

Joyce poked her head into the room next door, but saw that the woman there had a visitor sitting near the foot of the bed knitting something pink and frothy. Each room was like a person's hometown, full of mementos, wedding photographs taken during the war, children, grandchildren in sudden digital sharpness, books and crossword puzzles, until things had progressed too far for that. Then slippers and bathrobes vanished, clothes disappeared from the closet, belongings were swept away by relatives, the room pared down. Families often sat in vigil in bare rooms, all the photos gone. Perhaps it was too difficult for them to be reminded of a person's life at the moment when they had to begin to let go. She understood this because she couldn't bear to look at photos of Ruth as a child, the three of them in happier times. Colin had given her a box of negatives, but she hadn't been able to have them developed.

She went to the sunroom, usually empty in the winter, and looked out at the frozen river in the dusk. Beyond the ice, a narrow slit of black was opening, so cold and fathomless it made her shiver. She sat for a few minutes wondering if anyone had ever really been hers. Ferrall certainly hadn't been hers. She could barely remember his body, the body that had once seemed more real to her than all the accumulations of her life. And Ruth had punished her by shrinking her body so that it didn't look very different from the bodies of the patients she tended here, so attentively. People she might meet only once or twice, before they vanished completely.

Joyce remembered holding Ruth when she was a newborn, and losing herself in the timelessness, the hush of loving her, body to body. Nothing more was needed.

Before she went home, she checked in on Isaiah again. His daughters were still there and Jill was framing the picture of the dog. She must have had the frame all along.

George was feeding her father ice cream, but was leaving very little time between spoonfuls. Joyce could tell she'd never been around babies and had no talent for reading the rhythm of simple needs. He started to choke, deep hollow-sounding expulsions punctuated with little gulps. She helped George pull him forward, supporting his neck with her left hand. There was very little strength in him. The coughing exhausted him and he lay his head against Joyce's shoulder and nestled in quite naturally. His body was very warm and when they lowered him back to the bed, she shivered a little with the loss of his heat. Why was it that people seemed most alive when they would soon be gone? He smiled at her, a little of the rake left, and she laughed. A private joke between them.

. When his daughters left to catch the doctor before he entered the room, he said, "Come here."

Joyce leaned closer. She had picked up some sense from the conflict in the room that there had always been another woman, and another after that. He spoke to her almost under his breath, and she hoped he wasn't going to act out of habit.

"Is there any way you could spirit me away from here?" he asked. She was struck by his choice of words.

"I don't have my wallet, or my driver's licence. I don't know where they put my pants," he said.

"It's pretty cold out today. And the roads are icy," she said.

"Oh," he said. "Would tomorrow be better?"

"Maybe tomorrow," she said. One of these days, he would be gone.

"I have to take my dog with me."

"That's the great thing about dogs. They'll follow you anywhere."

"He's such a good boy," Isaiah said, concentrating on the photo of the dog then, cajoling, soothing, caressing in a voice too low to make out. Joyce knew she was leaving him in good company.

§

SHE CALLED RUTH THAT NIGHT. Colin answered, sounding in good humour.

"Joyce, we're playing music. Yasmin and Doug are here. Why don't you come over? And bring your flute."

This quality of forgetfulness, of resilience, had been aggravating when they were together. Now she recognized it as his particular talent for living. But she couldn't come over. Most of their friends had fallen away from her life. She had grown used to being alone and would have become disoriented by revisiting what had gone on without her.

Once she stood inside the doorway of her former apartment waiting for Ruth to come to the door. She had arranged a visit with her daughter, a formal request to Colin that had obviously not been agreed to by Ruth. She had heard the two of them talking urgently, too low to hear what was being said. As she had waited, she avoided looking too far into the place that had been her home. At her feet had been a new throw rug, orange and green, a colour combination she never would have chosen.

Lifting her eyes, she caught sight of a familiar sleeve, steel-blue with a band of Inuit embroidery, the two-part layered parka she had been wearing the New Year's Eve she had met Ferrall. She felt a bit light-headed, her heart giving two hard knocks against her chest wall as though it wanted to escape her and live again in this apartment, beat within that warm confines of that coat she had abandoned, along with her life. She was sure it must still be stained with the spots of blood from the cut above her eye, the cut Ferrall had tended that night she had become separated from her family on Parliament Hill. She had once left those blood spots there purposefully, brazenly. Winter would be coming soon, she had realized, and she would have to make a decision about whether or not to reclaim that coat.

Finally, she had not, and found another parka at the second-hand store. She was wearing someone else's history through the first winter she was spending alone. She could see its plum-coloured sleeve on a hook near the door as she talked with Colin on the telephone.

"Joyce?" he asked, and she realized that she hadn't answered him.

"Thanks for the invitation, but I just need to talk to Ruth for a minute."

Ruth took a long time to answer the phone and Joyce could hear the wariness in her voice.

"Are you finished dinner?" Joyce asked.

"Yes, Mom. I ate a half a side of beef, two suckling pigs and a whole apple pie."

Joyce laughed, but Ruth hadn't meant to be funny, only sarcastic. She had started eating again, had quickly regained her former weight. Joyce's absence had allowed her to give up her vigilance, but she was still angry.

"I was thinking of you today. I saw a little boy stamping in the slush with new red boots, rain boots for spring. And I remembered that night you wanted to be tucked into bed with your boot. It was new and had a cartoon figure up near the brim. Bugs Bunny, I think."

"I don't remember."

"I remember like it was yesterday."

"So, you called to reminisce about my childhood wardrobe?"

"No. I wanted to tell you that I'm always thinking about you. I miss you."

"That was your choice, your doing. Don't blame me."

Hearing her resistance and lack of trust, Joyce thought, good, she's not hardened. She hasn't turned and walked away.

WHEN SHE NEXT ARRIVED at the hospice, the two nurses on duty were moving quickly. The usual timeless quality was suspended because two patients were actively dying, and the hospice tried to make sure that they wouldn't be alone during this time. Isaiah was one of them and she went immediately to his room.

His breathing was strange, as though the automatic function had been turned off. Many people pulled inside themselves when this hard part began, but Isaiah spoke softly, as though in a dream.

"Blue … heart of blue … glowing," he said, so softly Joyce had to lean close to make out the words. Joyce couldn't tell if he knew anyone was there. She had been told that the daughters were on their way. This last vigil would be very painful for them and perhaps they were putting it off as long as they could. His eyes were closed. He might have been lying here whispering to himself for a long time. Colours, all colours, a pulsing generous spectrum was what she hoped for him.

She asked if there was anything she could do. Did he want company until his daughters arrived? She wanted him to hear her voice, know he wasn't on his own. Hearing was the last sense to go.

"My arm … so cold … "

She touched his arm, where the bruised stain of pooled blood had appeared since the last time she had been here, but his arm and hand felt warm.

He stopped speaking and fell deeper into himself and Joyce continued to sit with him and held his hand in the cup of her hand. Outside the window, winter was melting. The sun was lifting higher every day and a weak shaft of it angled across the foot of the bed. Something was different about the room. It already felt empty and then she realized why. His paintings had been taken down from the walls, but the watercolour paintings had not yet been returned to their hooks.

Then, the sun set, light suddenly fading, and shadows stood patiently in the corners, waiting to be asked to step forward into the room. Over the next half hour the walls, the bed, the empty shelves suddenly turned grey. She could hear a drip outside the window onto the flagstone path, irregular, three beats close together, then two spaced. A pause, then two beats again. No rhythm, a randomness. Yet Isaiah's breathing had a distinct pattern. His chest would rise as his breaths intensified, reaching a depth and then beginning to recede, breath by breath, until they stopped. She waited and after 30 seconds or so, a shallow breath would be taken again, each one even, although deeper than the last, until the largest deepest breath was taken again. This pattern had a name, Cheyne-Stokes breathing, and it could go on for an hour, or a day, or several days, until that shallow breath did not reassert itself in his chest and he would be finally still.

She closed her eyes and listened and it was like sleeping in a tent close to the sea. Like she was back with Colin and Ruth on the island of Grand Manan, listening to the waves as they lay in their little tent on a cliff above a herring weir. And then, when the tide was finally high, the sound of whales breathing in the middle of the night, surfacing and gently receding as they fed on the small fish milling about at the dark mouth of the weir. Such huge, calm breaths, with all the time in the world between them. Colin had put his arm over her and she held his hand against her heart, both too moved to speak. Ruth slept through it and they let her. This was something private between them

She opened her eyes then and watched Isaiah sleep. His daughters would be here soon and she would never see him again. But she knew from her own losses that there would be no completion even if she stayed in the room with him. He was rising and easing below the surface naturally, without effort now. His eyes seemed to be spaced more widely, there were shimmery movements beneath the pale lids, his mouth thinning and widening like the mild dreamy face of a fish. This wasn't exactly sleep, just as a newborn doesn't exactly sleep. Gently, between being here and being nowhere, she felt herself travelling with him and understood that she wasn't holding his hand any longer; he was holding hers.

Blood Secrets

"THERE'S A REASON I LOOK LIKE MY DOG," Dulcie said. "But I only figured out why after many years."

She was at a neighbourhood party, in the kitchen with women her own age. The kitchen had been recently renovated and they had been given the tour by the much younger owner to admire the changes, but stayed on after the hostess left for the living room where the younger crowd and men had gathered. The colour scheme was avocado and gold, just like the kitchens of her teenaged years, but with a brass space-aged hood for the stove and brushed chrome faucets. The sink was white enamel like the old sink at Graham's mother's farm. It was the sink that made her think of telling her dog story.

"Emma's a beauty, not like those stinky Labs. You could do worse," her friend, Kristin, said.

Her dog, Emma, was an unlikely choice for a small house in the suburbs, being a full-sized collie bred to run long distances herding sheep on foggy mountainsides. She had a flowing black coat, with the same wings of white streaming from her temples as Dulcie. They both had long sad faces.

"Labs are bad, all that shedding and farting and bad manners. If they were men, we wouldn't let them in the house," said a woman with short spiky grey hair. Dulcie didn't know her.

"Wait a minute, I want to know. Why do you look like your dog?" Kristin asked.

"Graham wanted a collie because he had one when he was a boy. He loved that dog," Dulcie said.

"Okay. I'm not getting it. What's the connection?"

Dulcie pointed at her black hair and said, "He chose me because I looked like his childhood dog." And everyone laughed.

"The most Freudian part of it is that she was named 'Ring'." She held out her left hand with the wedding ring.

Their laughter must have drawn one of the men into the kitchen, because suddenly Dulcie heard a deep voice behind her.

"When he calls you a bitch, it's a compliment."

The women closed the circle and ignored him and he left with a fresh bottle of beer from one of the coolers at their feet.

"Honestly, we're not safe anywhere," the woman said who'd made the comment about Labs. Dulcie didn't mind. She'd told this story before and there was usually someone recently divorced who couldn't resist the same barb. Telling this story in the face of mid-life cynicism was what gave it irony, an edge, a sense of how far they had come since those first days.

Later in the summer, she spent a weekend with many of the same women, at a cottage where they discussed a book and saw a movie based on the book. The end of summer had made them giddy, a little hysterical to burn themselves out on laughter. The book was *A Thousand Acres*, which they loved, but they turned the movie off around midnight in favour of skinny-dipping in the cooling lake. Soon, they would feel that old reflex to get the kids ready for school, even though the kids were going soon or already gone from home. As they swam, the musty green smell of fresh water seemed to be breathing directly into their open mouths, warm mist floating above the cooling surface. They told funny stories about their husbands, laughing the way they once would have, as adolescents. But they hadn't known each other as teenagers; they were mid-life friends, which gave them more freedom. Treading water, her breasts buoyant as they had been when she was a teenager, Dulcie took the dog story one step further. But it was still true.

"I thought it was because I looked like his childhood dog, but I actually discovered that there was another female in Graham's life during those formative years. Cosmo, the black milk cow. Every morning at 6:00 A.M., he'd lean his head against Cosmo's flank and milk her as he sang Leonard Cohen songs to her. That's how he wooed me too. He used to sing me to sleep."

"Would you rather be following in the steps of a dog or a cow?" someone said, treading water a ways off. It sounded like Carolyn, but she couldn't be sure. The cold water was clipping their voices, collapsing their ribcages a little.

"Depends. When Amanda was born, I was glad there had been a Cosmo girl before me. Graham taught me how to express my own milk. And I was desperate for relief in the hospital when my milk came in." She remembered the night sweats through the first few nights after giving birth, and the blood rushing, in a hurry to be spent after nine months held at bay. Not a gentle easing warmth like the tailings of blood in her life now, blending effortlessly, silently, invisibly with this cooling lake. How alarming birth blood was the first time, richer, darker, thicker than menstrual blood. And the way her breasts throbbed with hot tension, relieved only by giving of herself in a way that was new and strange.

"Ugh," her friends said, all around her, like a halo of reaction coming at her out of the dark. "He didn't, did he? Really?"

Someone paddled closer, breaking into the conversation.

"What? He called you a cow? He said you remind him of a cow?"

Dulcie, recognizing the voice, knew that this woman had been unlucky in her own choice of husband.

"I'm the one calling myself the cow. Remember those Jersey cow days? The mechanics are the same, only the scale is different. There's worse things to be than an animal."

Through the years, she had always preferred to be out rambling, pushing a stroller through sleet and freezing rain. Later, she would squelch through mud with Emma along the river paths, once her children were in school. All this wandering and pushing through urban thickets, and thinking, thinking, thinking, suited Graham. Perhaps what her friends had asked her was true. The footsteps she had been following were circuitous, informed by instinct—animal tracks along water, meandering heavily on soft spring days for the sweetest grass, or following a scent of something quick and wild. She did step into the imprints of these animals, Ring and Cosmo, and was glad.

There were other stories that came to mind that she hadn't told, even though they were on the same theme, and revealed more about how they had managed to go the distance of twenty-five years together. The children were gone, and they were returned to each other. Emma, too, had grown old and sleepy and soon would no longer agree to lift herself onto arthritic legs for a slow pass around the park across the street. So she would walk alone soon. Her friends had continued on, telling funny stories about relationships they had when they were young. She let the subtle current of the lake carry her a little away from the group, remembering that first journey she had taken with her husband.

THEY HAD HITCHHIKED to the bridge, crossed the black swift-moving river, and then walked the last five miles on country roads to the farm where his mother and younger brothers still lived.

The grey dusk, a kind of ugly sour colour against the paler snow, turned into a slick night of freezing rain. In the city, this kind of weather was an irritation, making people walk like Charlie Chaplan on the slanting sidewalks, but here, in the intense darkness, she was disoriented. All the girls her age, nineteen, were growing their hair long, and writing poetry about getting back to the land when they weren't baking inedible loaves of insufficiently risen brown bread. They had already decided that they would have natural childbirth and grow all their family's food themselves. And that the fathers of their children would be gentle with animals, delivering the spring lambs that never went to market.

But here she was, cold, wet, barely able to keep herself upright, while he walked just a little ahead of her to her left, as though protecting her from traffic, non-existent on such a night. She was annoyed at her own vanity, having refused to wear a winter hat. By the time they reached the fork in the road that he said was the halfway point, her long hair was clinking like wind chimes, Rastafarian braids of ice. She was intrigued by him, but not yet sure if he was worth this night of misery.

Through the first few miles, gingerly walking with her arms stretching out for balance, she wondered if he thought of her only as a friend. He was protective, true, but his easy nature and the way he led the way through familiar territory suggested that there was no erotic tension growing in him. Even when she fell, and he hauled her up by the arm, he didn't linger. But the tension was growing in her. His voice was sinking into her body as though she heard him through an inner ear in her chest. He was impractical, one of the few guys studying English literature, head in the clouds, often walking right by her in the hallways at the university. She knew he went home on weekends to help on the family farm, and that suited his beard, his loose jeans and the muscles she could make out under his work shirts. The strength in his upper body was gentle somehow, natural, a result of chores and long days out harvesting the fields before classes started, which was different in quality from the hard mean-looking muscles of the guys in her classes who worked out at the gym or played competitive sports.

She had worn a new Indian silk top tied with tassels at the throat, rich scarlet and purple and gold. The ice from her hair was melting on the back of her neck, running in little rivulets down her back and chest, between her breasts. She hoped the dye wasn't running, as it sometimes did with these inexpensive imports that she loved. There was a chance, a small chance, that he would see her skin tonight, the smooth firm breasts she was so proud of, and she would prefer to avoid anything vaguely comical, such as bands and stripes of strange colour branding her like a zoo animal. She could smell the incense rising from the shirt, even from beneath the wet wool smell of her coat.

Only later would he tell her that he couldn't remember her name. Her first name, Dulcie, of course he knew, but her last name had slipped his mind.

Years later he said, "It would have been all over for us before we even got started if my mother had wanted a formal introduction. As we were walking up the driveway, I was thinking, McDougall, MacDonald, McTavish. I had the Mc part down, but the rest—I had no clue."

"That was some formal introduction," she said. "Like something out of the movie *Deliverance*."

"Hey, hey. Watch what you say about my family. I resemble that."

§

THAT FIRST NIGHT, close to the farm, at the gravel pit glowing a fainter grey in the intense dark, he kissed her, with his hand slipping so naturally under her jacket to her breast. She had been slightly alarmed by that, but was also lost in those first tentative explorations of his mouth. Things had sped up over the course of a walk on a rainy night, and if he hadn't known her name, alarm would have overtaken attraction.

They turned into the long driveway. Only one light seemed to be on and Dulcie wondered if they were arriving too late for supper.

"Will your Mom mind meeting me this time of night? Has she been waiting?"

He laughed and said, "Ma doesn't know I'm bringing anyone with me."

"She doesn't know? You didn't ask her if it's okay?" Dulcie was horrified. This isn't how she imagined things at all.

"She likes our friends to come around. Don't worry about Ma," he said.

So that was it. They were friends, despite the kiss in the gravel pit.

Dulcie and Graham walked around the back of the farmhouse where Graham bent down to pet an old dog, that had been barking deeply, yet without much enthusiasm, since they turned in from the road.

"Hey, Pushkin. How's it going," he said to the dog, scratching it under its matted chin. Dulcie had never seen a dog this unkempt, with shanks of matted fur hanging off its thick black coat. Hay stuck out of its fur and it seemed to be smeared with mud, or was it manure?

"Do you let that dog in the house?" she asked and hoped he wouldn't catch the incredulous tone.

"Pushkin's an outdoor dog. She's a sweetie, the last of Ring's pups."

Pushkin curled up again on the muddy rag on the porch floor as they removed their boots. They entered the farmhouse through the back door, stepping onto a rag rug. Dulcie looked down the dimly lit length of the hall, ugly wood paneling, old tiles lifting from the floor. The house looked every one of its more than 100 years, but without charm. It had been cheaply updated in the 1950s. Eleven children later, the house was battered, electricity flickering dimly thanks to ice lining the power lines outside. And it was eerily quiet.

They reached the end of the hall and turned right towards the kitchen. In her peripheral vision, she saw something strange on top of a freezer—denim, plaid, coiled with energy. Before she made sense of it, two boy-men jumped from shoulder height onto Graham, yelping like wild dogs. Amazingly, Graham stayed upright and the three of them boiled in an exuberant male knot. One of them had his forearm locked around Graham's throat, practically lifting him from the floor. Graham was shorter than his brothers. Then, as suddenly as it had started, it was over, and Dulcie was introduced to Derek and Jimmy, the two brothers still living at home and running what was left of the farm after their father's death years before. Neither brother would look her in the eye, a bashfulness she thought then. But later the same trait allowed the brothers to drift away from the farm and family in the decades to come.

"BUT YOUR MOTHER was the scariest," she said later, remembering the sound of the chair legs against the floor in what used to be called the parlour, her heavy breathing, her snuffling, laden approach to the kitchen. She was wearing a handmade sack, patches of floral fabric, polyester and summer cottons cobbled together, over brown stretch pants. She must have been close to 300 pounds. Her hair was wiry, eyes small within the abundant flesh of her face, yet her lips were bright with red lipstick. And she had good cheekbones. She ignored Dulcie, rocking from foot to foot as she went to check potatoes boiling on the stove, slamming the pot lid, then aiming and landing in a chair close to an old wood stove.

The only thing she'd said to her directly, as Dulcie got up to set the table with forks, no knives to be found, was, "You a college girl, and that's the best you can do?' lifting her fleshy arm, indicating Graham. At first, Dulcie thought she was being criticized for the way she was setting the table. There weren't any knives in the drawer. And only bent spoons. Later she found out that they never had knives. Knives disappeared into the barn to fix hinges, or just disappeared and were dispensable.

She only understood that his mother's comment had been meant as a joke when Graham went to his mother, wrestled her head against his chest and kissed her grey hair.

"You love me, Ma. Admit it." She pushed him away, still not looking at Dulcie, but pleased. Her ruby-bright mouth was freshly lipsticked and her hair had been combed, probably when she heard the dog barking and knew Graham was on his way in.

The affection between them made Dulcie relax. After they ate fried eggs with the darkest yolks, like tropical sunsets, homemade buns, mashed potatoes and gravy, Dulcie and Graham went back to the barn to spread hay for the cattle. The cows either were pregnant or had calves.

"Do you need to milk them every day?" she asked, knowing nothing about farming but trying to sound like she did.

"You'd never freshen a herd of dairy cows all at the same time. These are beef cows. We just keep one for milk."

She helped him by gathering armfuls of sweet dusty hay and filled the trough, ducking between the cows. They frightened her with their mass, the weight they were carrying on their small hoofs. With just a shift from foot to foot, they could crush her. The straw hissed like fire in her arms, the crackling sound, not of sparks, but of bursts of summer tickling her nose. She felt satisfied when a cow immediately lowered its head and pulled the hay lazily through heavy lips, chewing as though it had all the time in the world.

Graham called to her and she emerged from between two brown cows to see him sitting on a stool with his cheek against a black cow, his hands gentle on her swollen side.

"This is my favourite, Cosmo. Do you want to feel her calf?" he asked her. She squatted beside him and he held her hands over the rough coat. There was a rolling movement, then a shape like a sharp fin gliding beneath the surface, and she jumped back.

"Whoa, Nellie," he said, laughing at her skittishness. And she moved towards him again, trusting him. The unborn calf undulated against her breast and she turned her head to tell him what she felt and he kissed her again.

He took her up to a bedroom facing northeast, with peeling violet paint over white plaster, where wooden boxes were stacked to the ceiling.

"This is the bees' room. You can sleep here."

"With the bees?" she asked, alarmed. "Do they ever come out at night?"

He laughed and kissed her forehead as he settled her into the three-quarter bed, lumpy, covered with a heavy handmade quilt made of simple squares of fabric, much like his mother's clothes.

No art in its construction, only practicality where nothing was wasted. She felt like a child being tucked away for the night.

"They're all asleep," he said. "That's my story and I'm sticking to it. The hives go back out in the clearing once things start flowering." He kissed her again and said, "No stings."

"Promise?"

"I promise. I'm staying in the other room," he said.

"With your brothers?"

"The boys' room. Yes. This room was for my older sisters."

"Where will you sleep?" She had only seen one bed in that room as she passed by.

"I'm used to sharing a bed." Then he looked away, suddenly shy. She thought he was a little worried about the intimacy they both knew was coming, in a week, in two weeks, soon. But later she understood that he had been confident and sure about their sexual life beginning. He was only ashamed of the poverty he came from. By bringing her here, even if he couldn't remember her last name, he had been affirming a choice he had already made.

The wind had picked up once the freezing rain stopped and the window frame whistled, mournful, eerie. She was cold, but if she closed her eyes, she smelled summer in the waxy sweet smell of the hives held in limbo. A faint musty smell, but unmistakably honey. Then he lay down with her and they kissed, body to body, although still fully clothed. The room continued to chill as the wind blew harder and he moved her so that the quilt was free to cover them.

"Sounds like wolves," she said. "That wind."

"It could be wolves as well as wind. They come out of the hills this time of year. Sometimes you can see them near the barn."

He turned off the light and pulled her towards the small window. Her eyes couldn't adjust to the country darkness. There was only the touch of his hand, the sound of his breath.

"They eat the afterbirth shoveled out of the barn. We're in the middle of calving season."

"Really? Nature can be gross sometimes," she said.

"More like not wasteful. This is a hard time of year for animals, and nothing gets hurt. Just your sensibilities," he said.

"I'm really not that sensible," she whispered to him, desiring him and quickly doing calculations in her head. She was a few days away from the end of her cycle and probably wouldn't get pregnant. Suddenly, she couldn't wait.

Mouths, hands, bellies pressed moist with heat between them. They kissed most of the night because to not kiss made her mouth feel strangely dry and bereft. They were slick with desire and satiation and desire again. She heard her voice, but it was not her voice. Her breath and his breath on her face in the dark filled her lungs perfectly. He filled her perfectly.

She woke before he did, just as the sun lifted above the barn, sliding into the violet room. Someone was starting a fire in the wood stove downstairs, but no warmth had started to rise through the grate on the floor. Then she heard a strange pounding sound like a fist repeatedly hitting flesh and the table legs creaking against the floor. It was a sexy sound and she slipped down further, nuzzling against his bare chest. The skin along her ribcage was fused with his, had to be pulled free to allow her to shift position, waking her further as the downy surface of her skin resisted and then tore free.

Then she noticed the dried blood near his armpit. Lifting her head, she noticed more blood on his neck, smeared across his chest. His sleeping face was stippled with blood. She lifted the heavy quilt and looked down at her naked body. Her torso and hips were blood-stained, too. Or was it red dye from her blouse? Across her chest was a stain, a bluer red than blood. But there was definitely a dried smear of blood on her left breast. She was a mess. The only pain she felt was a soft throbbing, a sunburn-like sensation between her legs, but satisfying, nothing ominous. Neither of them seemed to be cut. Then she was fully awake, finally realizing that her period had started, had probably been flowing strong all night, made heavier by her sustained desire. In the total blackness of night, her slickness hadn't seemed surprising. The aching knot deep in her belly had felt like the most intense desire she had ever experienced. And the result was this: when the sun came up they looked like hyenas after a frenzy. Horrified, she tensed and her throat clenched and held back tears, wondering how she could hide this, dreading him waking up. In his state of light sleep, he must have sensed an abrupt shift in mood and his eyes immediately opened.

He looked at her, alarmed, tensing and sitting upright in the bed. For a moment, she forgot about the blood and wondered if he didn't recognize her, but then she realized that her face, too, might be streaked with blood.

"I'm sorry," she said, curling her knees to her chest.

She looked at him again and saw that he looked frightened. It wasn't disgust, she didn't think. Quickly, she answered what he hadn't asked.

"No. It's not that."

"Not the first?" he asked. "I've heard for some women, it's tough. They ... "

"No. Don't worry. It must be my period. Oh, God, what a mess."

"I didn't want to hurt you."

"Did I seem to be in pain?"

They both laughed.

He told her to relax, lie in bed, he'd be back. Before she let him leave, she licked her hands and cleaned the blood off his cheek, the iron taste of it returning to her through her fingertips. His clothes covered the rest. He was gone longer than she expected. She heard a metallic rhythmic sound outside the window, like some reluctant soul being pulled up into the light. She heard him singing and realized he must be at the pump outside, filling the trough for the cattle. He called to his brothers who were working in the barn, "I'll be back." But still she waited. At least she had her backpack with her in the room and had been able to find a tampon. The sheets were bloodstained. She didn't know how she would be able to face his mother. Then she could hear him talking in the kitchen, and eventually, his footsteps on the stairs.

He was carrying a basin and facecloth.

"The sheets too," she said and suddenly started to cry. "Oh, I'm so sorry." She was also appalled, ashamed, mortified.

He sat next to her on the bed, held her face and kissed her nose, then licked it. Touched her left cheek with his tongue.

She pulled away. "How can you stand to do that?"

"Dulcie, you taste like dulse."

And with that, they belonged to each other.

They washed each other's bodies with the warm water he must have taken from the reservoir of the wood stove because it was rusty, even before the blood tinted it. They took turns with the cloth and her skin tingled with cold in the trails he left behind. She washed his feet even though they were clean.

"Appropriate for a Sunday morning." he said.

"Just like that slut, Mary Magdalene," she said. Because they were both studying English, they could laugh at the same references.

"Your mother would probably agree. How did you explain the basin?"

"I didn't."

"But what will she think?"

"What she already thinks. That you're too good for me. That you need ablutions because you're so pure and refined."

"But what about the blood?"

"She'll think I caught a live one. Good for me."

Before they left the farm to return to the city, they hung the washed sheets over the wintering hives to dry. Only the faintest stains remained.

HIS MOTHER NEVER MENTIONED the sheets in all the years that followed that weekend. When they stayed at the farm, it was understood that they would sleep in the bees' room. She always heard his mother kneading down the bread dough on the kitchen table, that warm sound in the kitchen that made her want to drag Graham back into the warm nest of the bed for another round of lovemaking. The wooden boxes were gone from the room after that first winter, and she had never seen them again, but the room still smelled like dry wings and honey to her. Just before the farm was sold and Graham's mother moved into a nursing home, Dulcie needed to spend some private time there, placing her warm palms against the cold sloping plaster.

She thought of this night over the years, but didn't tell this story to anyone for a laugh. She'd been tempted once, when a friend had described how she had thrown up all over her husband on their first date and the way he had tenderly cleaned her up and delivered her to her parents' door made her realize that she would marry him. The blood rite had been the same for her.

§

WHEN THE CHILDREN WERE GROWN, she felt a need to be connected again to something physical, something to do with nurturing, so she became a volunteer at a hospice. She worked Saturday evenings.

One night, she entered the room furthest away from the nurses' station. A man lay on the bed, his bones supported by carefully placed pillows. His wife was standing over him, holding his face between her hands. She looked to be in her late seventies, while he seemed ageless, the skeleton that would endure underground long after he was gone from this bed. She was murmuring to him and Dulcie waited before introducing herself. She was saying his name softly. "James. Do you hear me? James, I love you." She kissed his cracked lips and said it again. Dulcie felt like an intruder but couldn't turn around and walk out of the room without breaking the spell between husband and wife. But she was wrong about intruding. The wife, Gwen, knew she was there and lifted her eyes, smiling with something like mischief. Dulcie took a step back, shocked, but then she reinterpreted the look she'd seen as warmth, an invitation.

They talked easily about Gwen's life with James and he followed along with his eyes, watching first one woman, then the other. His mind wasn't clear enough to join the conversation.

Gwen held her husband's hand, telling Dulcie that she'd been spending nights in the room because her husband was afraid and wakeful between 2:00 and 4:00 in the morning. She was tired, but glad to have this time with him, alone, after all the busy years.

Dulcie thought of how strange it was that love relationships started with that wakefulness, that full engagement with each other's bodies in the middle of the night, then the middle-of-the-night needs of babies disrupting intimacy between husband

and wife, before entering a long sleep of daily life through middle age. She hadn't realized that the focus could flip, to the body and long nights again at the end. Almost as if a physical relationship was roused again in a different and even more intense form in old age. Even though he seemed to be emptied out, pale, bloodless. Death came on as a kind of gradual bleaching, the skin thinning and growing more dry. Just as her body was now starting to pale, her periods coming less frequently, and when they did, after an absence of months sometimes, she felt a melancholy for her lost fertility.

Dulcie offered to give James a foot massage so Gwen could take a break, if she wanted one. After being in the room a few minutes she'd realized that James needed touch to keep him settled. Perhaps the morphine was causing agitation. Gwen stood over her husband, once again with her hands directing his gaze to her own, and said clearly and slowly, "This woman will give you a foot massage. Would you like that?" He seemed puzzled by the meaning of these words, but then smiled at his wife and nodded.

Dulcie uncovered his beautiful white feet, so soft at the heels she could tell he had been in bed a long time, and began to rub lotion over the insteps, holding them firmly between her two hands and squeezing gently. He moaned and gave himself over to her touch. As she explored the toes and bones and gentle curves of his feet, she and Gwen talked about James's job as a small engine mechanic, their children and grandchildren, how they met in the lineup for a movie in 1950. James broke up a skirmish between two inebriated men and prevented Gwen from being knocked over.

Gwen held James's hand as Dulcie held his feet and he was included in the gentle drifts of conversation, as if his body were the current holding everyone together. Dulcie was moved by how comfortable Gwen was with another woman touching her husband in this sensual way, comfortable with how much he was enjoying another woman's touch.

WHEN SHE GOT HOME, she told Graham about the couple in the hospice. Usually, he changed the subject, restless in the face of details he was not yet prepared to think about, but tonight he was attentive. When she was finished, he told her about a couple he sat beside on a plane as he was flying back from Calgary the week before. A couple about the same age as they were, the man staring straight ahead, unmoving, and the woman sexy, with a scoop-neck red sweater, gold chain resting on the smooth skin of her chest.

"I get it. I get it," she said.

"This isn't about her attractiveness, although she was one of those straight-backed, high-coloured women, very strong and very small. You know the type—built for multi-day canoe trips and vigorous bouts of Saturday afternoon sex."

"Dream on," she told him. "So what's the rest of the story?'

"I thought they were estranged, the husband was so unresponsive."

"Ah, the rescue fantasy."

"No, I'm serious," he said, a little sharply, so she let him tell his story unimpeded. He told her that the woman was obviously terrified of flying, buried her head in the stony man's shoulder as they banked, gasping a little when the landing gear bumped up inside the airborne plane. But then he heard a murmuring from the man, a soft grunt, almost under his breath, although he didn't turn his head towards his wife. I thought, "How cold can a guy be?"

After a pause, which Dulcie left uninterrupted, he continued.

"She had her arms, both of them, looped through his inert arm. It was strange." Graham said.

"But I had it all wrong. Once the meal came, she calmed down, and started to feed him, bite by bite, one spoonful for him, then a spoonful for her, then him. I noticed the braces on his hands and knew he had some horrible thing like Lou Gerhig's disease."

"You don't live long once you're that sick. A year at most."

"I know. The strange thing is that they were able to communicate without words, Without his being able to do anything at all, he could comfort her. And for a minute, I found myself feeling a little jealous."

"Jealous. Why? Do you think I couldn't do that for you?"

If they had been younger, this would have been a cue for them to head to bed and reassert their claim on each other. Instead, they sat quietly, side by side. She wondered if he was thinking the same thing.

She reached out and took his hand and although he didn't answer, she felt the warm pressure of his fingers responding to her, as if by instinct and habit. He was preoccupied with his own thoughts. Maybe he hadn't heard her at all.

"My father never had that. Neither did my mother."

"Had what?" she asked.

"The chance to face it together, to falter and fade and be kind to each other in different ways. She was folding laundry as he lay on the bed after morning chores. They were talking, about nothing in particular, nothing important. He stopped answering and she turned around to see why, and he was dead."

"That's awful. I used to think that was a good way to go, but now I'm not so sure. Your mom always talked about him as though she'd see him coming through the door tomorrow."

"Right to the end, she was sure she'd see him again. Ring wouldn't let the undertakers take his body out the back door. She went crazy, so they had to back up and take him out the front way.

We never used that door and the glass cracked trying to get it to open."

"I remember the cracked glass. I remember seeing it that first weekend."

She saw the glass in her mind's eye, a fractured prism in the brilliant sunlight that cleared away the freezing rain of the night before. A luminous web, and it made her remember the smell of sleeping bees and damp cotton spread out over wintering hives, the secret blood fading in the sun that was strengthening by the day.

Stone Deaf

THE FLIGHT WAS UNSETTLING. Pressure changes worked their mischief in his ears, deadening sound. He swallowed hard. He had every reason to feel apprehension when sound suddenly dimmed, like tunnel vision of the ear. Both his parents had been deaf: his mother from birth, his father from a bout of meningitis at 18 months. Although he knew their deafness wasn't something he would instantly manifest at the age of 44, he felt marked for silence all of his life.

But it was more than that. The flight was unusually quiet. No one around him was speaking. He wondered if he had missed some cue of danger that others had picked up. He looked beyond the husband and wife sitting between him and the window and saw nothing strange through the small oblong window. The plane had lifted above the thin layer of vapour, gentle white hands hovering just above the warm layer of thick atmosphere. They were flying level now, in constant calm sunlight just above the hands. The jagged mountains, sediments thrust into the sky, were retreating in a line away from Calgary, all sparkling and new in the morning sun. In a few minutes they would leave even that connection with earth behind. He could barely see the perfect squares of prairie far below, scraped bare by glaciers from the last ice age and pocked with lines of ground water. He didn't want to lean further towards the man beside him to see more. He could never be sure of the appropriateness of his physical closeness to strangers. His parents had been very physical in their communication with him, and even now he wondered if he had properly learned the non-verbal cues of the hearing.

He rose and turned after the seat belt sign was turned off. The silence suddenly made sense. Half the plane was occupied by a group of deaf travelling together. Some were kneeling backwards on their seats, signing to the people behind them. Hands were flying, faces mobile with sudden smiles, raised eyebrows. The hearing people all around them were conspicuously still, faces buried in books, but he could tell by how some of them leaned slightly away that they were uncomfortable with the gesticulating going on around them, as though it was somehow infantile or unseemly.

As he walked towards the washroom, he could catch snippets of what they were talking about. They had made arrangements to take the elevator up the Peace Tower in Ottawa at noon, when the carillon bells ring the full twelve peals out over the city.

"You'll be the only ones without hands over your ears," he signed to a middle-aged woman kneeling on the seat.

She reached out and grasped his shoulders, laughing, and asked him with her hands if he was going to the conference too and if he was from Calgary, why hadn't she ever met him before.

"I'm hearing," he said. "But I grew up in Ottawa and know the Peace Tower well. My mother took me up to feel the bells many times when I was a child. It was one of her favourite places."

The woman put her hand over her heart at the mention of his mother. "Your mother was part of the deaf community?" she asked.

"And my father."

"That's why you're so fluent," she signed.

"Yes, but it's been a while since I've signed." They looked at him expectantly, bracing themselves to hear that she was dead, this extraordinary woman who brought him, a hearing little boy, to feel the most spectacular bells in Canada. And they were right in a way. His mother was extraordinary, both his parents were, especially for the Sixties. His father managed every work day to negotiate the world.

His mother was unabashed about taking him out into the world. She would defiantly stand beside him in stores, her steel-grey eyes glittering, as he interpreted her sign language to shop-keepers. And once the large department stores and supermarkets opened in their neighbourhood, she took to them because then she wouldn't have to ask anyone for anything, ignoring the stares of people around them as she surrounded him in a flurry of signed conversation.

"She lives in Cape Breton now. She's not well. I'm on my way there." He was given a hug and heard a murmuring around him, a kind of toneless murmuring. It was comforting. He felt exiled from this old world of touch. Over the head of the woman who was embracing him, he saw one of her travelling companions—a sullen stocky man in his early thirties who glared and turned his head away. It was a polarized community. Some thrived, as his parents seemed to, and some grew alienated, dulling their loneliness with alcohol, as his mother came to finally. Living in silence, as his mother was now.

Over the past few years he started to suspect she drank from her strange syntax over the telecommunicator, which was their main means of keeping in touch. The mechanical voice that translated her typing was nothing like her, and he was slightly disoriented when they spoke on the phone, keeping their conversations brief. When he was younger, he would have had good instincts about her, would have known she was all right. But as an adult, he was never sure. She made it difficult in her old age by resisting change, never having taken to email, even though he bought her a computer. Sending her words off into space, she called it, but he wondered now if it was a sign of a larger rejection. Her retreat to Glace Bay might have signaled something ominous.

WHEN HE ARRIVED in Sydney, he rented a car and drove to his mother's small house in Glace Bay to drop off his baggage before going to the hospital. It had been a mining house, quickly erected in the 1920s, half of a shingled building a block from the crumbling cliffs. Its roofline was shaped like a mountain, peaked in the middle, a strange place to divide two self-contained living areas. Her side was painted a bright lilac, clashing with the emerald green of the other half. He remembered his mother asking him when he was a boy of eight or nine: "Can you hear the colour of that lilac bush?' Because she had never heard, she never really understood the limits of sound.

"It's whistling, like a kettle," he said to her then. He remembered how happy she seemed with his answer. He could see that it felt right to her.

He had never understood why she had moved back to her childhood town after his father died. She had left Glace Bay when she was seven or eight to go to a special school for the deaf in Halifax, so she had no friends there. Older family members were dead or suffering from dementia, and distant relatives had never learned to sign. All of his cousins had moved away. As far as he could tell from their phone calls she was quite alone there. The telecommunicator had a built-in delay as her words were converted, so he couldn't read her tone.

"Are you sure you're not too lonely?" he had asked.

"I have my mother and father."

"But they're dead," he said.

There was a pause.

"At a certain point, there's no difference. Your Dad is dead too, but I talk to him every day."

He wondered now why he didn't ask her more about what she hoped for and what she needed at this stage in her life. The pause enforced by their telephone conversations only made tangible the barriers that had slowly grown up between them, as he was increasingly pulled into the hearing world. Because he and Valerie had not had children, there had been no pressing reason to fly across the country to visit, so they had seen her for brief weekend visits, flying in and out of the Sydney airport, three or four times a year since his father had died.

It wasn't enough. At times, he felt an acute longing for her, remembering how she could recognize a fifth on the piano by placing her hand on the wooden cabinet. He practiced like that, with one of her hands on the piano and one on the back of his neck, as though she was the conduit for the music coming out of his fingertips. And he would feel proud of her when she sat on the floor at the foot of the bleachers, so supple and young with her long brown hair. He played basketball in high school, and she came to all his important games while his father was at work, her girlish feet bare so she could feel the excitement of the audience and the quickness of the play through her soles.

But then there was loneliness for him too, as he grew older. When he walked out the door in the morning, he had to adjust for how everything around him was suddenly muted, as though he was the one who was deaf. People never looked one another in the eye. The flickering light of moving hands in his household, vivid as sunlight on poplar leaves, was almost entirely absent. As he entered the awkward stage of adolescence, he could go for days unrecognized, unacknowledged. Rarely did anyone look at him in the open, direct way he was used to at home, straight on, their eyes and mouths and hands moving in an animation of what they were trying to communicate. In time, he learned that dulled-down language too. His signing at home slipped down to his waist, confined, as though his hands were locked in a tackle box.

"Speak up," his mother would sign, jutting her hands up and widening them level with her chest, fingertips near her chin. But he would shrug and walk away.

And she let him go. He only realized how far at his father's funeral. Even there, back in Ottawa, the wake was segregated, hearing from deaf. His parents' deaf friends staked out the area around the open casket, their flying hands touching each other's shoulders and faces, ready hugs and tears accentuating his father's stillness. Many of them verbalized as they spoke, gruff or wavering explosions of sound. His father's hearing friends and colleagues from the government, where he had been an editor for thirty years, kept back and spoke softly, without gestures, to one another. His mother had entrusted him with the task of moving between the two groups and he was surprised at how tiring he found it. After years of living in western Canada, he wasn't used to moving from one culture to another, from muted voices and neutral facial expressions to unabashed tears and gripped shoulders.

One of his father's government friends, a woman about his age with intricately knotted reddish hair and the whitest pallor in the room, took him aside and asked him to show her how to say, "I'm sorry for your loss" in sign language. He saw her a few minutes later practicing clumsily in the corner, her back turned to the room, then showing several other people, who were even clumsier than she was. Somehow they lost the concept of "your loss" so that by the time they reached his mother, they were saying to her, "I'm sorry for you." She greeted that with a frosty restrained smile. By that time, his mother had grown quite militant about being part of the deaf community and didn't appreciate any suggestion that she was somehow disabled.

SHE HAD BEEN TAKEN from her house quite suddenly when the stroke occurred three days before. She had managed to dial 911 and when she didn't speak, they sent police and an ambulance. Although she must have wanted to be saved, she had not communicated with anyone since she was brought to the hospital. One nurse knew a little sign language, but his mother hadn't responded. When paper and pen were put in her good hand, the one they knew was unaffected by the stroke, she drew irregularly shaped circles. When she drew perfect ovals, she smiled a lopsided smile that was not directed at the outside world. He had gotten to Glace Bay as fast as he could. Valerie had driven him to the airport that morning.

"Do you have anything you want me to say to Mom," he had asked her at the airport.

"She's never been able to hear me. That's not going to change now," she said, looking down at her still hands in her lap, as though suddenly embarrassed by how blunt she had been. But this forceful way of speaking had been part of what draw him to her. Then she turned and kissed him, whispering, "Godspeed."

He knew what she said was true. They had married urgently more than twenty-five years ago, when they were too young to care about either of their families attending. They were living across the country, in Edmonton, where they were graduate students. So much of their lives together revolved around talk, the witty banter of their friends, words lobbed back and forth like a tennis match. And talk was their livelihood. Both of them taught at the University; he in Classical Studies, Valerie in English Literature. Valerie in particular was a quick talker, a dynamic teacher, and had never gotten used to the telecommunicator they used over the telephone to keep in touch. Speaking slowly enough for the translation to appear on the screen at the other end of the line never came naturally to her. He knew, though, that what didn't come naturally was his parents' acceptance of her. His mother would have loved the term *profoundly deaf* if she had ever been able to hear it. For her, deafness was an inspired silence that gave her and others in her community a sensitivity to touch that Valerie could never be part of.

HE HAD ONLY STAYED at his mother's house in Glace Bay once before, just after she moved in almost ten years ago. Every other time he visited, she insisted that he stay in the hotel along the highway and he took her out to lunch, dinner, to Sydney to shop, spending very little time in her increasingly disorganized house. That first time he had stayed with her, it had still been uncluttered and full of echoes because she hadn't yet put curtains up. As was their habit, she signed and he signed while talking out loud so it was only his own voice that he heard bouncing coldly off the unadorned walls. She had been excited by the move from Ottawa to Glace Bay, something that he couldn't understand. The town was dilapidated, the commercial strip adorned with false 1940s two-storey fronts leaning precariously in the strong November gales. They had been put in place by a famous movie director years ago, when he made a film about his own years growing up in The Bay. Perhaps he had left them behind as a gift to the town's rough-and-tumble past, but they were flimsy, temporary, and gave the town an even more down-at-the-heels look. Store fronts and two old wood churches were boarded up, with crows living in the belfries. The sea, which could be seen from his mother's bedroom window, was muddy, brown cliffs crumbling, stained red in places as though they were leaking blood.

"My mother would have a fit if she saw me living in one of the miner's houses," she signed to him. "We had a beautiful one on Main Street. I'll show you."

They had walked there in the afternoon. The house stood close to what had become a busy road, its cedar shingles now painted the grey of the sea. It had once been grand, with a glassed-in porch. But the windows were dirty, the steps unpainted and flaking away. That was the feeling about the whole house, that it was tired of standing.

A young woman came out of the front door and looked alarmed to see them standing on the front lawn near the place where the peonies had been. When she saw his mother signing, she backed up to move inside again.

"My mother was born in this house," he told the woman, hoping that she would offer to show them the inside.

"I'll get the owner," she said and closed the door. A young blond man emerged with a shaved head.

"Been here 8 months. Nothing's changed since then," he said, staring at his mother, then looking at him when he spoke. "The ceilings used to be high. But they redid them."

He knew then there was no point in going inside. It was apartments now, renovated in a cheap and ugly way. He asked the young man if he minded them going into the back. It was stark, devoid of trees, mostly a car park. But he could see that it had once been a beautiful garden. There were angles and nooks and corners. The carriage house was not painted grey, but had once been painted a peach colour that was mostly worn away.

His mother signed to him quickly about the roses, lilacs and mock orange her mother had grown, the hammock in the summer, and the car with a rumble seat where you could feel the wind hit you in the face. She didn't seem interested in looking inside, but he put his eye to the crack between two doors, drawing back when he was blinded by light. Walking around the back of the carriage house, he realized the whole back end was bashed in, wrecked.

She led him around the side of the house and showed him the coal chute, unused now.

"Blue smoke lifted from all the chimneys in the winter," she told him. "Coal is very colourful. Black and shiny in the cellar. Crimson inside the furnace."

She told him that coal created her father's livelihood although he never got his hands dirty. Coal brought the men and money, and they needed entertainment, so first he opened a Nickelodeon, and then a vaudeville theatre. She loved the animal acts the best, the dogs, wearing little suits and bowties, jumping through hoops. Then came the silent films. By then she could read and missed nothing, with her bare feet propped against the piano as her older sister played the accompaniment.

"My father told me coal turned into diamonds. I thought I wasn't reading his lips right, but then he told me how."

"What did he say?"

"Press this long and hard enough and you'll have diamonds. But the poor fool who lets it slip through his fingers will get nothing but a lungful of black dust."

"So did you try?"

"I believed him. My father had a face like the best performers. You could read everything on the surface, or so you thought. I went down to the cellar and took a piece of coal to my room. I put it under the heaviest book in the house, the Oxford Dictionary. All night I thought of my coal lying under words I loved and words I hated and words I would never hear, even if I lived to be a hundred."

"And in the morning?" he asked, knowing the answer, but letting her finish the memory that was obviously so vivid.

"I had a lump of coal and a dirty dictionary," she signed, and laughed with her breath and eyes only. She had always refused to vocalize, even though it had been the philosophy of the more recent schools for the deaf to teach this technique.

"The talkies came in after that and I couldn't understand them as well. Then they decided I had to leave home. For school."

"That must have been hard. You were just a child."

"I missed them, but they needed to send me away."

"Does a child understand that?"

"Now I do. Because they let me go, I was able to go to Gallaudet University and meet your father. They gave me my own kind, my own life."

Then what was she searching for by returning to her childhood home? Her parents had been old when they had her, and they died more than half a century ago. Her sister had died a few years before. What did she hope to find? She seemed so excited about being home. Everywhere they walked in the small town, she was able to tell him what stood before, how things looked when she was a young child. Her visual memory was so vivid, the past seemed more real than the present.

They went inside the theatre her father had built, and rebuilt more than once after a succession of fires. Each time, it reflected the age it was constructed in, ending its natural evolution as a derelict movie house that showed mostly Westerns and porn. But in the 1980s it had been taken over by the provincial government for its heritage value and returned to its 1920s glory days, a neoclassical performance space with plaster columns and elaborate ceiling designs. A red curtain framed a dramatic wide stage.

"Yes, this is the same, but the colours are different," she said. "The decor was gold and rose. And the stage curtain was painted with a scene from ancient Greece."

They were the only people there. Hard times had continued and there was little entertainment coming through town. The stage, when they climbed the stairs from the orchestra pit, was dark and dusty.

WHEN HE ENTERED her house, where she had lived the last ten years of her life alone, he was shocked at how it had changed. What little furniture she had was old, mostly junk from second-hand stores, but the small house felt crowded. There were glass bottles everywhere, wine and spirit bottles stacked neatly under the bathroom sink, all along the walls. The inside wall that joined her home to the one next door was a solid mosaic of bottles stacked with their bottoms facing outwards. The sun was angling into the room and caught the glass wall, but dimly, since it had travelled the distance of the house. The glass lit up with dark jewel colours, quite beautiful, but he sensed that this collection had nothing to do with aesthetics. His mother must have been unwilling to discard the bottles along with her trash. He never before realized that she was sensitive to being talked about, as was inevitable all her life. She had refused to feel ashamed of her deafness, but a drinking problem was something else, something she wouldn't want the town to whisper about, even though she couldn't hear what they would be saying.

The countertops, window ledges and tables were covered with stones she had gathered from the coves near her house. She favoured round stones, all sizes. Some were green as eyes, others red, striated with porous black layers. Some were black and looked as though a painter had dribbled white paint in thin lines on the surface. One stone was purple with blue flecks. There were hundreds, if not thousands of stones. The effect of the bottles and stones was of a home that was a snag of coastline, where detritus was washed to shore by storms. What am I going to do with these stones when she dies, he thought. The bottles he could throw away, but the stones she had chosen, one by one, for their beauty and had carried them here to keep her company. He couldn't imagine hauling them in buckets to the cove and emptying them into the sea.

He talked to the nurse before he sought out his mother in her room.

"As the doctor told you on the phone, it's hard to tell how much function she has. The scans look good but she's unresponsive."

The nurse paused, and then added, "You do know about her complicating condition?"

"Her deafness?" he said.

"Of course you know about that," she said and smiled at him. She was a lovely woman, middle-aged with dark Celtic eyes and pale skin. "I mean her drinking problem."

"I'd suspected."

"She had to be given Valium the first few days to control the tremors. That might have flattened her affect. But it's also not unusual for people who've had strokes to be depressed. Does she have any family or friends here?"

"Not that I know of," he said, feeling like a terrible son to be so absent from his mother's life.

The nurse reached out and lightly touched his forearm.

"That's not that unusual either. Don't be too hard on yourself."

Her touch released the tears in him and she gave him a minute before she took him to his mother's room.

His mother was lying in bed, washed out and pale as the sheets. Her hair had grown completely white since he'd last seen her. Or perhaps she had recently stopped colouring it. Strange, the things he didn't know about her. He came close to the left side of the bed and held her hand, her dominant hand and, luckily, the hand unaffected by the stroke, but he wouldn't have known this because it didn't respond to his touch. Unless she turned her head and focused on him, there was no point signing. He looked through the window beside her bed and could see a curve of the town's beach and the sea, riled up and steel-grey. He put his other hand on her forehead, stroked her hair back. She didn't move or acknowledge him, didn't look at him, so there was no opportunity to say what he had rehearsed. Still, he stayed the afternoon, quietly reading beside her bed.

THE NEXT DAY, the heat was closer and more intense, more like what he remembered from his summers in Ottawa than a town on the cold north Atlantic. He walked downtown, passing the theatre on his right. He noticed that a new glass lobby had been built where there had been two boarded up stores, so that the theatre looked more expansive. The cramped doorway was gone. Some of the boarded-up churches were also gone, but hadn't been replaced with anything new. They were vacant lots. He walked towards the chronic care home, but wasn't ready to go in yet. He continued on, following the road until he came to the cemetery where his grandparents were buried. Many of the gravestones were so old they couldn't be read. Old or new, they all faced inland, towards the town their descendents had left, turned away from the ocean that today was deep blue streaked with pea green, muddy near the cliffs.

It took him almost an hour to find their graves. The first, a salt-white stone, glittered in the hot sun: *Connor Handel, born August 12, 1876, died April 3, 1957.* And next to him, a polished black stone, much smaller, but crowded with words: *Sarah McPherson Handel, beloved wife of Connor Handel, born September 9, 1884, died July 23, 1957. She will be missed.* Hands were carved below the dates, but not in the traditional prayer position. When he realized that the right hand, with its index finger pointing outward, formed part of the sign for *always*, he knew his mother had come here and arranged the stone for her mother. He only had a vague idea of when his grandparents had died and now he realized that it was almost a year after his birth in the spring. Neither of them had ever seen him, his mother had once said regretfully.

There was a space beside the two graves. His aunt had been buried in Hamilton and he realized he was standing on the place where he would bury his mother, probably sooner than he'd imagined. Something had drawn her back to this place, something stronger than the memories she shared with his father. He would let her rest here.

By the time he reached the care facility, his shirt was drenched with sweat and he was thirsty. He drank deeply at the water fountain as the nurse he had talked to the day before came by.

"How are you?" she asked. He stood up and felt his head spin a little from his walk in the hot sun.

"You look like you've seen a ghost," she said. "You're awfully pale."

"I think I have," he said. "I went to my grandparents' graves."

She smiled suddenly.

"Your grandfather built the Savoy, didn't he? As kids, we used to go to the Saturday afternoon Westerns."

"I never met him."

"Neither did I. He was long before my time, but I loved his photograph in the lobby. He looked so dashing with his thin mustache. We thought he must be famous. His portrait was signed just like a movie star's."

"I just found out that I was born before they died."

The nurse waited, giving him space.

"My mother used to talk about how she wished they had had a chance to hold me. She was lying."

"You can't know her reasons. Times were different then. People didn't travel as much."

"She could have just told the truth."

"Maybe she was telling a kind of truth. Maybe she wished she had been there for them. Time can pass awfully quickly, especially with a new baby. Mostly we don't know when it's running out."

"How is she today?"

"The same," the nurse said. "She's not communicating. I know a little sign language. She doesn't respond. The strange thing is I put my head in to check on her while she was sleeping and she was signing. She must have been dreaming. At least we know now that she can move her right side."

She was still sleeping when he took a seat beside her bed. He put his hand on her forehead and smoothed her hair to let her know he was there, but she didn't move. Her hands were quiet at her sides.

He hadn't brought a book, so he opened the drawer of the bedside table and took out the Bible. "In the beginning was the Word ... " he read. Yes, that was certainly true, even though sign language didn't break down all meaning into discrete words. One person speaking with another through their bodies alone. How he began; how each person began. He thought that to speak this way is to be caressed, to be held in a nurturing cocoon. Then he became afraid of sounds they couldn't hear: a siren one street over, a cat fight in the backyard, the crack in the ceiling of the house on the coldest nights in winter.

Her lifted his eyes from the page he wasn't reading and found that she was awake and looking at him. He reached over and took her hand and they stayed like this for a long time.

By late afternoon, the room started to darken, too early for twilight to arrive in July. He could see through the window that the sea was tossing steel-grey over green. The wind had risen and a fever was rising in the room. His shirt was sticking to his skin again as though he was exerting himself. His mother's hand in his was still cool, her eyes steady and neutral. But when the first flash of lightning lit up the room and the thunder was so loud it shook the building, she brightened suddenly. Looking around her with a kind of anticipation. The thunder sounded again and again. She wouldn't hear the wind, or the sharp rain pelting the window, but the thunder reached through her indifference. She watched the streaked window, him, the walls where darkness and light were flashing. He remembered how she loved thunderstorms when he was a child, would sit with him on the front step as the atmosphere thickened and the wind started up. They would run inside after the first thunder that was close enough to bring rain. And she would laugh her soundless laugh, all jagged breath.

When the storm was over, she still seemed alert.

"Would you like to go out?" he asked her, not knowing how possible this would be.

"Yes," she signed with her left hand, the first language she had used since he arrived.

It was complicated, and involved a special wheelchair with a neck brace, two people to lift her into place, but the nurse he had talked to arranged things. He pushed her along a boardwalk outside the facility to the beach.

He moved around to the front of his mother and asked her, "Do you want to go further?"

Again, she answered yes. So he pushed her onto the sand. The beach was lined with black residue, soft coal dust, and the wheels of the wheelchair were mired down, but still he pushed, moving them closer to the water. The waves were moving in one at a time now, spaced out and rattling on the small pebbles like the breath of someone sleeping. The storm had lifted coal dust from the ocean floor so that each wave stood up black before cresting with pure white foam. All around them the stones on the beach were still wet. Then the sun cut out from beneath a heavy cloud and lit them up, green, red, purple.

"Stop here," she signed, and he sat beside her, catching his breath. He picked up a stone, still cold from the rain. It was a swirl of layers, soft red and green, the colours still so close to the organic matter they once were, silting through sunlit water, compressed, then broken and polished to smoothness. The stone warmed in his hand and he turned to offer it to her. But she didn't reach for it. Instead, she reached down and touched his hair. She stroked his head, and he looked at the stones beneath him and absorbed her touch.

Snow Moths

SAKINA CARRIED A TOMATO into Andy Glover's room, but it was the wrong thing to do. He grimaced and turned his face away from the table on wheels where she had placed it like an offering. He was terribly pale, washed out by the sheets, the white venetian blinds, the dirty white walls. The only colour in the room seemed to come from the tomato and the Kaposi's sarcoma, purple welts on his neck and right arm.

He reacted to the movement of her arm as she reached to lift the tomato and place it to the side. He turned his face towards her again and said, "In one of my past lives, I was an apothecary. Nobody ate tomatoes back then."

"People didn't eat tomatoes?"

"No. They're poison. Like deadly nightshade. You heard of deadly nightshade?"

"I guess so."

"Same family."

"Oh," Sakina said. She couldn't think of any other way to respond.

"Girls would come to the back door. Girls in trouble. I mixed them up something strong—deadly nightshade, a little valerian to help them sleep through it."

"Where was this?" Sakina was confused. He didn't look like a medical person. He was missing one of his front teeth and a tattoo of the sign of infinity was poking out of the sleeve of his hospital gown.

"I don't know. A long time ago. In England, or maybe Germany. They started burning us earlier there. They caught me in the end."

"Who?"

"The men in skirts." He snickered. "I don't remember the fire when they'd had enough of me, but fuck, I remember the fingernails. They pulled out my nails one by one."

He held out his hand and she saw that he had fingernails, although they looked brittle and pale as the rest of him, with a hint of purple where the white moons should be.

She reached out and held his hand. "You're so cold," she said.

"Better than fire. Better than fire," he said, closing his eyes. She stayed there holding his hand.

Sakina was only one day into her internship at the nursing home, and this was her first encounter with Andy Glover, a young man dying of AIDS. She had just started the second year of Social Work at the community college, having transferred her university credits from England the summer before. Her supervisor had told her that she had been selected for this assignment because of her Moroccan background and ability to speak Arabic.

The neighbourhood where the nursing home was located was seedy by Canadian standards, but familiar, more like her home in Birmingham than any other place in Canada, which seemed deserted and overly private. There were many small shops, prices advertised in Arabic script, their produce lining the sidewalks in boxes: green and red peppers, gnarly branches of ginger, the deep blush of pomegranates vivid under the low November sky. Although she didn't read Arabic, she liked to bargain in her mother tongue, cajoling the shopkeepers, lobbing, catching and tossing back prices, just short of insult. No matter what price was decided on, the shopkeepers always added a few extra tomatoes to her bag. It was one of these tomatoes she had carried into Andy Glover's room.

She sat, feeling slightly ridiculous holding his hand, so she turned away from him to look around the room. She found his sleeping face too vulnerable. She wondered if she should reach over and put the tomato in her pocket.

WHEN HE WOKE UP, he smiled at her.

"My name is Sakina," she told him. "I'm a social worker in training. I'm here to help with any family things you might need. Or just to talk."

"No, you're not," he said.

"Not what?"

"Your name's Constance. Even classy ladies like you come to my back door. I saw your carriage out by the churchyard, curtains closed."

"That's just my English accent you're hearing. I haven't been in Canada long."

"Ah, Constance. It's okay. It wasn't your fault."

"I'm sorry. Did I do something?"

"Take it easy, Connie. No blame here."

He closed his eyes, his breathing deepened. For a few minutes, she sat watching his bony chest rise and fall, then she slipped away to talk to the nurses.

While Andy Glover was sleeping she came to understand from the staff that the Muslim patients had plenty of family around them. The real need for her was in keeping Andy Glover from calling out to every nurse who walked by, disturbing other people, even visitors of other patients, with his wild stories of past lives. He pushed the button constantly, and the light was usually lit above his door. He had been on the street for no one knew how long, had been a junkie and probably a sex trade worker before the lesions made him a pariah in the shelters and back alleys. Now he was dying. He had no visitors, no next of kin, yet he clearly had a great need to talk. Maybe she would be able to find a way to connect him to his own past, to calm him down.

The sun was gone as she put on her winter boots and coat for the walk home and, finally, she could drink and eat. Observing Ramadan in Canada felt easier than it had in Britain where the interval between sunrise and sunset seemed longer. In the hallway, she bent over the water fountain and drank in the musty cold water, tasting of caves, cisterns and secrets. It was an old fountain, recessed into the stone wall, and it was dark, like poking your head into a dungeon. But the water slid down into her empty stomach in a long tingling line like an icy scarf. The sensation stayed with her as she stepped out into the dark evening. Cold surrounding her, cold within her—she felt pure.

Josh was there when she got home, took the bag of tomatoes from her as he kissed her and she imagined their ripeness squashed between their chests, the stain they would leave.

"Dinner's ready. You must be weak."

He thought Ramadan was a hardship and was solicitous, making sure that hot food was bubbling away on the stove before she stepped in the door. This had been his way even when she wasn't fasting, and she felt a slight flare of annoyance. They were still getting used to each other after a long-distance courtship conducted mostly by telephone.

Two years before, she had had a car accident, and he wrote to her in England, having heard about it from her friend, whom he had met when he was backpacking. He started to call regularly during her stay in rehabilitation. During that time, every person in her life was deeply focused on her body, noticing how much she drank, how well the bone graft had taken. Cranked up in a lift, she was bathed by the nurses, their washcloths bristly as the exposed hair between her legs. Her body belonged to the world. Once she could eat again, her mother spooned soft food into her mouth. Her aging mother sat beside her on the bed, tending her body as though she was a child again, an old woman dragged back to the cradle. Even her own voice had been made harsh by the breathing tube left for three weeks, threaded down through her larynx, into her lungs. Her mother sang softly to her, old Moroccan folksongs, and she knew those songs were lost to her. Only a rasp remained that eventually softened to a normal speaking voice, but she would never sing well again.

When she was in the hospital, Josh had seemed like fresh air she could draw into her aching lungs, pure voice on the phone. He was words on the page sent from a place unmarked by her losses. She had felt the pull away from her family, and interpreted that pull as having something to do with him.

Her parents had let her go, and she had joined him in Canada last spring, once she could walk easily again without a limp. She had been a change-of-life baby and her sisters were already married, living close by, with children. Although she did know that the quiet way they agreed to her leaving had something to do with her accident too. Her mother, having almost lost her, was protecting herself. But she was already gone. The three weeks she had spent in an induced coma to give her brain a chance to heal had sent her off on a journey, searching for something she would never find close to home. Maybe it had been Josh, but gradually over the six months she had been in Canada she had started to wonder if she had made a mistake. She couldn't get over the strangeness of his physicality, the way he had been waiting all this time for her in the flesh.

"Does it hurt?" he had asked soon after she had arrived, touching gently the scarred line of red along her thigh where the stitches had been. They were getting to know each other the old-fashioned way, like an arranged marriage in which suddenly they were intimate and strangers at the same time. She told him, no, not anymore, lifting his chin so that he would look at her face, but he stopped again at the scar on her throat where the tracheotomy scar had grown silvery. "I wish I'd been there for you."

"You were," she had told him. "Your calls reminded me of something outside of that awful room."

"But I wish I'd been there in that room for you," he had said. "So many scars. I didn't understand how badly injured you were. I mean I knew intellectually, but touching them makes it all so real. I'm sorry I wasn't there."

"You were there in the way I needed you to be," she said, trying to pull him back to the present. After being forced to focus on her body for two years, after the hard work of rehabilitation, she just wanted to move on.

JOSH KISSED THE END of her nose and said, "A drachma for your thoughts."

"That's Greek money, not Moroccan." He was always making comments like this, reminding her of how different, how exotic, she was to him.

"Okay. You're a million miles away."

"Sorry, I'm a little distracted by a man at the nursing home. He has no family. No one at all."

"That happens to too many old people in Canada. Not like your culture." He tended to romanticize her family background, but she ignored what he said and continued.

"But he's not old. He's as young as we are. He told me my name was Constance. That I turned him in to the torturers 500 years ago. And that he forgives me."

"You torture my heart every single day," Josh said. "I forgive you too."

She laughed, but pushed him away, and then to make amends, she asked him to do her a favour. Even though she knew she shouldn't, she asked Josh to help her track down Andy Glover's family. And he was eager to help her, give her whatever she asked for, even if it was the life of a stranger. Against all the rules of her profession, she gave Josh a few details: birth date, middle name, and he was off to his computer like a bloodhound. It would give Josh something to focus on besides her and maybe she could use the information to help Andy Glover.

"...OUT ON AN ICE FLOE. They're gone," Andy Glover told her when he opened his eyes after waking from a brief doze. Sakina had been sitting at his bedside, watching the grey November light fail at the dirty window and wondering how to broach the subject of his family. How could she make him care about who he really was?

In the last week, he had told her about being sacrificed and put in a bog in Denmark, about being grabbed at night and locked into the hold of a slave ship in Africa, being tortured by Mengele at one of the Nazi death camps, about being one of Michaelangelo's apprentices and carving the left bicep of David. He said that the muscle had taken three months because he'd had to practice muscle after muscle following the Master's specifications, on little chunks of marble before he was allowed to touch the real thing. And every night he had an education in male flesh. At first he was unwilling and cried from the pain of it because he was only a child, but later he was willing. Then he could carve the male form perfectly.

Sakina had wondered if all these stories of past lives were metaphors for what he had really experienced. Living on the streets and fending for himself the way he had, must have felt like being buried alive. Or did the stories speak to his earlier life—the shadowy life with his real family?

At the same time, he was clearly growing weaker from opportunistic cancers growing unchecked by his failed immune system. Now he needed nurses to change and reposition him every few hours, and he slept restlessly, mumbling often and moving his head from side to side. Day by day, his bones seemed to be sharpening, his flesh consumed by fever dreams and visitations by the most horrific events in human history. She wanted him to be free of at least these nightmares, these terrible past lives, to give him some peace.

"What colour were your mother's eyes?" she asked him, trying yet another time to anchor him in something tangible.

"Black. You couldn't see anything but black."

"But you're so fair. Were you adopted?"

"I remember how black her eyes looked out there on the ice, when we had to let her go. And then my turn came when I was old. She was there with me after they left. The ice is really blue. You think you should be able to see right through it, but you can't. Not until the end. Then her eyes were watching me. Her eyes were on me until everything faded away."

"Did you grow up in the north?"

"I lived there once. It's not bad, you know. My mother was left on the ice. And me too. You just fall asleep. Easier than this way."

He'd never referred to his coming death before. She thought maybe he was ready to say more.

"What about your own family?" she asked him.

"I've had so many."

"Were you a foster child?"

Andy Glover just lifted his hand and swiped it dismissively through the air—the biggest gesture she'd seen for days.

"Let me ask you this—how will you talk about this life when you're gone, when you're in the next one?"

"Some lives are there to hold a space open. I'm just killing time," he said and grinned, but it changed immediately into a bitter grimace. "Or maybe I'll remember some dark angry bitch not letting me move on and asking me all these stupid questions."

She was offended by this, but realized that if she were a psychiatrist, she would probably be pleased with this little display of pique. She must be getting to him, so she pushed on.

"Don't you want to remember, maybe see someone from your family before you go? I feel I should talk to you about this."

"I've seen plenty."

"There must be someone..."

He looked at her then, and she felt restless and nervous suddenly with his gaze. Then her stomach rumbled from hunger. He heard and smiled bitterly. He hadn't eaten in a long time because of the thrush infection in his throat.

"Somebody else wants something," he said as though it was an innuendo.

"It's Ramadan. I eat after sundown."

"Do you pray ass-over-teakettle on one of those little rugs?"

"No. It's more cultural for me. I grew up fasting. I like it."

"Why?"

"I feel free. And clear."

Then he closed his eyes and said quietly, "That's just how I feel."

FREE AND CLEAR. That's what he said he felt on his deathbed. As she walked home, she tried to imagine that. Her own experience had been very different, although she did realize that she no longer feared death. Life seemed so much harder than death. Of the accident, she remembered little. Only that she had reached down for a bottle of water and somehow skidded out of control. She didn't remember the ditch or the tree and only bits and pieces of the four hours she was trapped in the car as they sawed away metal, chunk by chunk. During that time, she was worrying about a new wicker side table she had been transporting back to her friend's apartment, hoping it wasn't damaged. And her shoes were gone. They were new shoes with pointy toes. Where were they?

There were shadowy shapes outside the glass, but the sounds of their voices, one asking her, "What is your name?" over and over were muffled, as though through water, but her name was irrelevant. She accepted that she couldn't move her leg. Even her left arm was pinned and she kept trying to move her head to make sure she could see if her favourite ring was still there. She accepted her body being trapped with great patience while worrying about her shoes, a plastic bag of vegetables in the back seat, the CDs scattered on the floor.

All through this time, one or another of the busy people outside the car distracted her from these important thoughts. "Tell me your name." "Do you know your name?" The glass was broken and a hard disintegration rained down on her, but the figures were no clearer, only louder. The pain came later, unbearable pain surfacing every time her mind lifted into semi-consciousness.

Someone had been there with her the whole time. A man with sandy hair, sitting in the chair at the head of her bed, and bending at times over her, close to her face, she remembered the sweetest-smelling breath, like jasmine tea. She remembered his voice and the touch of his hand, the outline of him blurry against the overhead lights. The way he stuck by her, attentive to her with the most incredible love. He made her feel safer than she had ever felt in her life. She asked for him once they let her rise up to consciousness completely.

"I'm here every day. There's no man," her mother had told her. She was angry, sure that her mother wouldn't let him into the room now because he wasn't Moroccan, wasn't one of them. All her sisters had married other second-generation immigrants from Morocco and Algeria and she understood before her accident that she would probably do the same.

"Why won't you let him come? I need him," she told her mother, desperate.

"I'm here all the time," her mother replied and Sakina could see her weariness. She asked for him every time she woke up from sleep but her mother truly didn't seem to know who she was talking about. It was impossible to accept that he hadn't been real. The hardest part of her recovery was giving him up. She knew she hadn't completely succeeded. Josh wasn't enough like him and that was the problem. She knew she was holding that against him. Which was unfair because he had no idea what standard he had failed in her heart. Only her mother knew about the man, and after a while she learned to keep this secret from everyone, not wanting the constant reminder that he had never existed.

JOSH WAS EXCITED when she got home.

"Look what I found," he said, giving her a file folder of Andy Glover's family. "They've been looking for him for almost ten years."

There were printouts of photographs put in the newspaper of Andy as a boy, springy blond hair, unruly, and the same scar on his cheek. There was his family then, and now, essentially the same but for his absence. Middle-class, living through a normal progression of events in another city: births, graduations, weddings, grandchildren, family reunions. And the plaintive messages sent out through newspapers looking for him, along with photographs. Hilary and Jack Glover still lived in the same house in a distant city, just as they had when Andy ran away. Every year on his birthday, April 23, they put another personal message in the newspapers across the country telling him this. Obviously, he had never responded.

Sakina's call to them was heartbreaking. First joy, then grief when they learned how ill he was. They wanted to fly in to see him right away. Sakina told them she needed to prepare him for a visit but they were adamant. They were on their way.

SAKINA STARTED TO EAT again that night. At midnight, Ramadan was over and she and Josh prepared a feast that lasted into the small hours of the morning: lamb and prune tagine, squash, date and almond rice, salads, apple cake and a turkey with all the North American trimmings. They had never cooked a turkey before and laughed every time they opened the oven door, twisted the leg and discovered that it was resistant, pulling back against their hands as though it still had a will of its own.

"This bird wants to fly again. It will never be done," Sakina said.

But eventually it was. After the apple cake and ice-cream, at 3:00 in the morning, they ate the tough bird by candlelight.

"I don't need this," she told Josh. "Any of it."

"You missed Thanksgiving dinner with my parents. I'm not going to let you get away with that. You live here now."

"Do I?" she said. The strangeness of sitting in this kitchen with him struck her.

"And at Christmas, I'm going to teach you all the jingles and carols."

"Oh, I already know them. Impossible to escape."

"... walking in a winter wonderland ..." he sang. "You couldn't really know what that's like. Just you wait."

"Why do you always assume that I don't know anything about being here?" she said, surprised at the anger that flared in her too-full stomach. As he cleared the table silently, she watched him, not rising to help. Who was this man? He wasn't familiar, or not familiar enough, despite his solicitousness. His voice wasn't right, and the way he was moving around the kitchen wasn't right either.

By Tuesday morning, she was sick to her stomach, probably from all the food she'd eaten in the middle of the night after a month of fasting. Something transient, but irresistible, and the metal rod that had been put into her leg to help it heal after the accident was aching in the bone. Josh was at work for the day and she would be able to sleep privately, quietly. She called the nursing home to tell them she couldn't come in. After she hung up, she remembered that she hadn't told the nurse coordinator about Andy's parents planning to see him as soon as they could get there. But thinking about how persistent he was in his refusal to say anything direct about his own past, she thought maybe it was just as well that they would make contact without giving him a chance to put up defenses. Later still in the day, she admitted to herself that she hadn't cleared any of this with her supervisor from the College and now it was too late. The next day was a holiday, Remembrance Day, and she wouldn't be able to talk to her until after that. It could wait a day, she decided. Andy Glover's parents didn't know when they would make it across the country. She would let it unfold as it would and be there on Thursday to help Andy Glover put his past together.

The government building where Josh worked was closed for the holiday and they had planned to take a rare mid-week walk into the hills north of the city. Even though she still felt a little weak and the pain was still throbbing slightly in her left leg, they set out. As they moved higher into the hills, the air clamped down, steely-cold. They rasped through dead grass with their boots, their breath swirling around their heads and lingering behind them as they walked. Cold crept in under her hat, making her nose run, and it tingled along her earlobes. If this was the beginning of winter, what would it be like in a couple of months? Josh seemed to be reading her thoughts.

"Do you mind this? The darkness here, winter coming?"

"I'm used to gloom. To rain and fog, but cold...I don't know what that will be like."

"Can you make a life here?" She knew he could only ask this because he was looking down at his feet and not at her. She felt a sudden pity for him and the way he had been competing all this time against a man who had never existed. That man had been comforting, Josh was comforting; that man had sat at her bedside and kept her company through the darkest nights of her life, just as Josh would if she needed him to.

They walked from luminous hardwood forest where the bare trees put up no resistance to the sky and into the low light of evergreens. The wind was suddenly gone although it was no warmer. Her breath rose around her face, the icy smoke of it riffling along her eyelashes. Frozen leaves cracked like crystal under each foot. All sound was underfoot. The ache in her leg had gradually faded as her muscles had warmed up. The sky was breathing easily, the awful rattling of the leaves gone. She felt quite calm.

"That's what I've been trying to do," she told him and he let her stop there.

After a while she noticed white lights fluttering up from the dead leaves underfoot. At first she thought she was seeing snowflakes, but squatting to take a closer look at what would be her first glimpse of Canadian snow, she realized they were tiny white moths stirred up by their feet.

"Josh, what are these?" Their wings had a slightly shredded outline. "How can they live in such cold?"

"They won't make it through the night," he said. "I've never seen them before."

They had to be warm—little sparks too late for food, or sex or eggs, rising from the leaves only to show themselves alive this last time.

Then flakes of snow really did start to meander here and there through the air, corkscrewing down and landing on the frozen ground. Soon, they couldn't tell which white flecks moved deliberately and which were moved by the light wind. The difference between the snow and the moths dissolved.

"Snow moths," she said. "Amazing."

How sad, she thought, that this is how it would end for them. Flying, then frozen, lost in the snow as though they had never existed. An accident of timing, perhaps, led them to this. Just as she had been led to Josh. The pieces of her life were still flying from the velocity of that accident: some things would be shattered, some would be retrieved and put somewhere new. Josh would be part of what shattered once it landed. She didn't know how she had not understood this until now.

"I do love you, Josh," she told him for the first time, knowing that she would be leaving him soon. "Whatever happens, it's not because I didn't love you. Always remember that."

BEFORE SHE REACHED his room, Sakina found out that Andy Glover had died. One of the night nurses met her in the hallway on her way home. She was clearly exhausted and didn't tell more than this fact. The senior nurses had left by the time she reached the station, but one of the older practical nurses was still there. She was someone who had scowled at Sakina initially, probably not liking the look of her black hair and brown skin, but once she'd heard her voice, her English accent, she'd adopted a confidential, gossipy way with her. She told Sakina what a crazy night it had been. Sakina half-listened to her, more intent on checking the records to find out if Andy Glover had had any visitors the day before.

But the practical nurse wanted to relish the details and wouldn't let her read. She told her in a low voice about how he had cried and thrashed around, trying to get out of bed all night. The older nurse complained, "We're not even allowed to have railings on the beds anymore. Well, let all those high-minded bureaucrats spend a night keeping a dying man in his bed and see if they change their tune."

Sakina felt queasy hearing this.

"What happened? He was so weak last time I was here."

"We could have used you here last night, let me tell you. He was so much easier to handle once you started coming around. Last night, he had the strength of Goliath. And swearing. You never heard such swearing and carrying on. It took two nurses to hold him and give him a shot to calm him down."

"So, what happened?" she asked. "Did something in particular happen to set him off like this?" She couldn't bear to be direct in her question, but the nurse didn't pick up on this, instead continuing on with her blow-by-blow description of Andy's death.

"He must have worn himself out," she finally said, concluding her story. "As soon as he stopped fighting, he passed away. The undertakers were here about an hour ago. We haven't cleared the room. If you know someone who might want his things, go ahead."

She was afraid of what she'd done. It was only a matter of time before she would have to admit what she had set in motion. In a minute, she would ask about contacting his next of kin, and then she would know, and do her best to make things right, at least for them. But she needed a quiet moment first.

She opened the door and sat on his bed. The sheets were stuffed into an overflowing hamper beside the bed and the hard plastic mattress was cold. Her body's warmth would soon make it comfortable and then she would sit and sit, unable to leave this spot, to stand up and walk out of this dingy room. So she got up and looked around the room for his possessions, whatever they were. If his family had come yesterday, there would be some clue, something they left behind. But there was nothing except what the nursing home provided: terrycloth bathrobe she'd never seen him wear, skin lotion, mouth swabs, half-full glasses with bent straws. What things did the nurse mean? She wanted something of his to remember him by, and pulled open one drawer and then another, but they were all empty.

Where All the Ladders Start

S HE EMPTIED A SHELF of books into her backpack, shifted them around so that the sharp corners wouldn't jut into her spine, and slid into the harness. Her husband, Luke, was holding the weight in the air as she adjusted one strap, and then the other, snapping the two together across her chest.

"What did you put in here? Rocks?"

"The Bible, all five volumes of the *Collected Papers* of Freud. And my old high school biology textbook."

"You surprise me. No novels. All work and no play?"

Deirdre smiled at him. She knew that beneath this banter, he was genuinely worried, so she tried to keep things light to reassure him. "*Paradise Lost. Heart of Darkness*. Does that make you happy?"

"If you're going to be weighed down by baggage, you might as well make it the whole history of Western thought."

Then he released the weight and her vertebrae contracted with the shock of it. Automatically, her breath was pushed out of her lungs and her knees almost buckled with a panicky weakness. The feeling was familiar. She had been very ill throughout the winter and the more weight she lost, the more leaden she had seemed. Through the coldest months, she had not stirred much from her bed. Noise, light and movement had been too disorienting for her to be part of the world. The icy tick of snow against the window had mirrored the static in her head.

But now it was early summer and she had almost regained her strength. They walked together through their neighbourhood, and she carried the backpack strapped tight to her body. She planted each foot in its hiking boot squarely on the asphalt. Kids playing on their front lawns stopped throwing a ball and stared. Neighbours waved, looking curious, but not wanting to stop her to chat with such weight on her back.

"They probably think I'm leaving you," Deirdre told Luke.

"Maybe they think I'm escorting you to the edge of town. Good riddance."

She laughed. It felt so good to laugh with him again. Throughout the winter, he had brought her drinks she couldn't swallow, tried to coax her downstairs for a change of scene, lay with her as her tears soaked the front of his shirt.

She sighed, remembering. Ever vigilant, he reacted to the sound she made, moved behind her and lifted the weight from her shoulders.

"Let me carry that. We have a long way to go to get back home."

"No. You won't be there with me. How will I get stronger? I don't think there'll be either gentlemen or sherpas on the West Coast Trail."

"Are you sure you should be doing this? You're still not back to normal."

"I may never be back to normal. What is normal anyway?"

"You know what I mean. This might be too much, and Zoe will be the one who has to deal with things if you're not up to it. Is that fair to her?"

"She's been planning for this all year. It's not fair not to go. I'll be all right."

THEY WALKED ON QUIETLY. She had to concentrate on her breath, one in for every second step of her left foot. Although she tried not to let on to him her doubts, she didn't know how she would negotiate eighty kilometres of slippery headland. The trail had been built in the nineteenth century for survivors of shipwrecks dashed onto the rocks by Pacific storms. They would complete it in eight days— up and down ladders bolted to the sides of cliffs, scrambling over boulders between surge channels, balancing their way across gullies and small ravines on fallen tree trunks, pulling themselves across rushing rivers in small cable cars. The backpack was so heavy that she started to see spots in her field of vision. She reminded herself of all the hungry and shivering survivors who had been forced to stumble along treacherous headlands without the help of ladders or boardwalks or maps. When Zoe had returned from Vancouver for her grandfather's funeral in the fall, she had said, "We should still do the trail. It will be something for you to look forward to."

Deirdre had been touched by her daughter's care. The funeral had been brief, a simple Catholic mass, with no visitation before, no reception after. The blunt fact of her father's suicide, finally successful after three attempts, had silenced everyone, even the priest, whose sermon only focused on the gospel, with routine platitudes about loss and forgiveness. Her father had been barely mentioned.

After the funeral, she went back to her parents' house where she had grown up. The tasteful suburban houses along the street still looked new, but the trees had matured, making the light more ominous than it seemed in her earlier years. Shadows at midday, while she remembered a sun so hot and bright on the front lawn that she used to have to construct a tent out of an old sheet so she could stay outside reading a book. She always felt a need to be out of the house. The house was sad, too many things unexpressed, just as it was on the afternoon after they had buried her father in a grave that was still unmarked. She wondered if her mother would ever get around to arranging for a headstone or if the fact of his death, or even of his life, would slip away into silence, as was the habit in her family. To escape the shame she, her mother and brother seemed to feel when they met each other's eyes, she had gone down the basement steps to the room where her father had spent much of his time. No doubt there were still bottles of rye hidden behind the furnace.

THE LAST TIME she had descended the stairs, only a month before he died, he had been there. She had brought dinner to her parents, nothing home-cooked, just the Chinese takeout that they liked. He hadn't answered when she called from above, so she started down to find him. She had been greeted by framed photographs of young men on a table at the bottom of the stairs, hair combed back, wearing black robes of graduation. Similar photographs were framed on the desk across the room. Her father's easy chair and television sat between the two sets of photographs.

"Who are all these young men?" she had asked him, and he turned towards her, alarmed. Then he recovered his composure, smiled at her.

"We all went to St. Francis Xavier together."

"You've kept in touch with all of them?" she asked, surprised because she had never seen the photographs or even heard him mention his classmates before. But she noticed that he had recently begun wearing his school ring, with the ominous black X raised on the gold, visible from across the room. Like he was marked and found wanting. He must have dug the photos out of the old storage trunk with the broken hinges. Although they didn't smell musty. The frames looked new, silver and gold, probably from the Zellers close by. She was sorry that she had come downstairs. Obviously, this had become a private space where he could feel safe with his inner life that had no place in the upstairs life of her family. So she was surprised when he answered.

"I read about them in the newsletter. These ones are dead," he said, pointing to the table holding the largest number of images. "And these are still alive," indicating the photos on the desk.

"I move them over from the desk to the table when I see their obituaries," he added.

When she reached the bottom of the stairs after his funeral, she sat in her father's chair between the living and the dead. Her father's photo was not included in either group, even though he had been trying to die intermittently since her late childhood. She felt his absence for the first time, and realized that he would never be here again. It occurred to her that she should find her father's graduation photo and place him with the dead before the pattern he had created was swept away, his clothes, photos, books boxed up and given to the Salvation Army. It was all anyone could do for him now.

THEY CAMP AT PACHENA BAY. She is still a little light-headed from all the travel, first across the country by air, then a quick sleep simmering with dreams followed by a ferry, then a van shuddering over logging roads. The beach, headlands, tall hemlocks and Western red cedars are silvery and unreal. Mist moves from the ocean onto land, dissolving the tops of trees that are leaning away from the indistinguishable void of water and sky.

They set up their little dome, purple and turquoise, assertively optimistic. Zoe seems to be watching her, which is an improvement from the obvious shock at her mother's appearance when she met her incoming flight. They walk along the arcing beach of the softest white sand, composed of millions of shell fragments. The swell is slow and gentle.

"You didn't tell me how sick you were this winter," Zoe finally says. Deirdre has been waiting for this since the day before.

"I knew you didn't want to talk on the phone for long. I thought you were sad after what Grandpa did. But you've lost twenty pounds at least."

Deirdre first thinks of minimizing things, but this hiking trip will be too challenging. They will have to be able to trust each other and rely on one another.

"I didn't want you to worry."

"Maybe I should have been worrying more. Maybe I should have come home."

"I wouldn't have wanted that. I know how things go with this illness. It's a matter of waiting it out."

"Grandpa didn't wait it out."

Deirdre hears the little girl in Zoe's voice—the little girl of three she was when Deirdre had her first episode of major depression. Deirdre, herself, at that time, couldn't believe that the terrible static in her head, the restless, sleepless zombie-state that had quite suddenly overwhelmed her wasn't a fatal illness, which it was eventually for her father. She had made it through the worst sadness of losing their second baby. Just when she should have been able to turn her attention outwards again, the illness hit her hard, and she literally couldn't stand up for weeks.

The nursery school teacher had told Luke that Zoe had repeatedly asked her, "Is Mommy all right?" The reassurance she was given only lasted five minutes before she would ask again. Once, Zoe had escaped the church basement where the nursery school was, climbing the stairs and making it out to the street. She was found by a woman passing by on foot. Zoe had been standing on the edge of the construction site, looking down into a deep hole in the road where giant backhoes were unearthing ancient pipes. The woman who found her brought her inside and yelled at the teachers for their carelessness, her loud voice making Zoe wail the way heavy machinery had not. A report had to be filed. She could have been killed. Deirdre knew, though, that it was really her fault. Zoe had been trying to get home to her, to make sure she was all right. Her worry was so intense, Fort Knox couldn't have contained her.

"No, he didn't wait," Deirdre says. "But he wasn't a patient man."

THE NEXT MORNING, they fold and roll and press everything into place in their packs, find a stream and filter drinking water for the day. They prop their full packs onto a fallen tree, waist high, and secure them. The weight is still daunting, but feels lighter than the books. All the things they need, clothes, dehydrated food, fuel and shelter, mold to her body better than anthologies of poetry.

She did the preparation for the two of them, measuring out and packaging everything in zip-lock bags. As she was counting mango slices, Luke had reached out to grab a slice from her neat piles and she slapped his hand.

"What will you do when Zoe begs, '*Please, Sir. I want some more.*'"

"I'll slap her hand too," she said.

"Spoken like a true mother," he said and they both laughed. But she was determined to do this well, carry only what they would need, nothing extra. She had taken the winter off and had only this to concentrate on. She hadn't yet reached the point of health where she could lose herself in one of the books she had loaded into the pack for practice.

They weave through a maze-like wooden entrance designed to stop all but hikers. Then they do it again, freezing in mid-step to take each other's pictures crossing the threshold. Action shots, holding their feet at weird angles, laughing. Then, finding a rhythm, they walk side by side. The first day of the trail will be the easiest. They follow what used to be a dirt road that is returning year by year to rainforest. The air is warming by the minute and wraps them in a lush blanket of scent, fungus and moss, green exhalation.

"How did he do it?" Zoe asks.

"Who?"

"Grandpa. You never told me what he did to himself."

"I didn't want that image to haunt you. I wanted you to remember him alive."

"Mom, that wasn't so great either. What I remember is the food dropped on his shirt. I remember him sleepy and drunk."

Deirdre still doesn't answer.

"It's harder when someone just vanishes. They are there and then they are not, with no reason," Zoe says. "I need to know, to complete it in my head."

Deirdre knows this only too well. She thinks of the daughter they lost, Lily, born when Zoe was close to three. She had been with them such a short while, Zoe didn't even seem to remember her. Just a few weeks, when Deirdre found her still and unbreathing in her cradle. She had overslept a feeding, it had been Deirdre's sore breasts leaking into the sheets that woke her up that morning. She carries this sensation with her from her other daughter's short life, this painful weeping from her chest, and the heaviness of the still body in her arms. So much heavier than she was in life. There, then gone, called back into nothingness as though her whole life had been a mistake.

"Do you remember Lily?"

"Mom, you're changing the subject. Of course I remember Lily."

"What do you remember?"

"Her little fingers closing around my finger. The way she could cry so loud I had to put my hands over my ears. I could remember that morning, but I don't choose to."

"You can choose?"

"I can try."

"Your Dad can do that too. It's just as well that you take after him."

They stop talking for a while as they climb a hill. The trail has become twisty, with roots snaking out of the ground and across their path, so they have to watch their feet. Veils of gently waving moss hang from the branches. The forest is heavily layered, life upon life, life upon death. Never has she seen such a profusion of greens. Moss growing on the sides of trees like tree spirits emerging face first, ferns sprouting high above their heads in the forks of branches, nurse logs, bumps of fungus covered over with soft green. They pass by the amazing open invitation of the skunk cabbage, up to their knees and wide enough to swallow one of them, huge emerald leaves spread wide.

"There could be dinosaurs here. Everything's so oversized and tropical," Deirdre says. "Some of the ravens circling overhead are as big as pterodactyls. I hope they're not hungry."

"Well, I am, although it's not because of this lovely aroma." Zoe squats next to the skunk cabbage, poking the huge waxy yellow flower with its spiked warlike centre stalk. "These remind me of the plants that spawned those slimy pods in that horror movie."

"*Invasion of the Body Snatchers*. All those innocent tendrils sending out feelers."

"And then watch out. Nobody is who you think they are. That's the scariest part. The way people can sense strangeness but be unable to convince anyone else."

Deirdre notices that their conversation, no matter how casual, circles back to the same things. Disappearance, the strangeness of fate, forces stronger than intimacy. How difficult it is to know or trust even those closest to you.

Ahead, they can see intense light, an opening in the rainforest showing blue sky and sunshine. Under the tall canopy of Western red cedar and the younger hemlocks and firs waiting for a chance to plunge upwards and plug any hole created by a storm, they can't see for sure that the cloud and mist have cleared.

They emerge onto a freshly cut lawn sloping down toward three white clapboard houses. This is the first lighthouse on their route. The 1950s orderliness of the bordered flower gardens of petunias and marigolds, the chain-link fence and gingham curtains hanging in the windows make them squint, being such a shock after the humid dim humming of the forest. Children have set up a table and are selling lemonade and home-baked brownies, but the prices are exorbitant and they're not carrying much cash.

"This is surreal," Zoe says.

As they pour their drinks, the children tell them they live here year round, can walk the ten kilometres down the trail to town for groceries if they want. There is also a helicopter landing pad for emergencies. They say summers are fun, with all the hikers passing by.

"Don't you mind being alone here?" Zoe asks the children. "Don't you wish you could go to school?"

"Oh, no," the oldest boy answers. "This is our school." He waves his arms in the direction of the rainforest pressing in on the little enclave of suburbia.

"That's the pioneer spirit," Deirdre says.

"With a little Donald Trump thrown in," Zoe says once the children are out of earshot. "They must make a killing with hikers. Nobody has room to carry empty calories in their pack, but that little taste of heaven … Especially since it takes you by surprise."

They sit at the base of the lighthouse sipping their drinks and finishing their brownies, looking down on sea lions sunning on the rocky headland below. Every so often they hear one of them bellow.

"He drank his death."

"Grandpa?"

"Yes, poison, in the garage."

"What kind of poison?"

"Herbicide. He cut it with ginger ale, and drank it out of a glass. Maybe it felt more natural that way, given that he always drank to escape."

"Did he mean to?"

"Yes. He was leaning against the wall, just feet away from the kitchen door. He could have easily crawled to the door if he changed his mind."

"Did you see him?"

"Yes."

Zoe accepts this quietly.

"Their house was just like this," Deirdre says, sweeping her arm across the short grass and boxed flower gardens of the lighthouse keeper's home. "Everything looked so orderly and under control. But dig down a little…" She trails off. Talking about this so frankly still feels wrong, even though Zoe has insisted. There are details Deirdre cannot tell anyone, especially her daughter. The way his body had tried to expel the poison, even after it was too late. Her mother had not entered the garage, having put up walls to defend herself from this years before. One look from the threshold was all she needed before she called 911. But Deirdre needed to see that it was over. Three times before she had hovered on that edge of life and death with him, seasick with grief. Somehow the toxins had cleared from his blood and let him live. They had all continued on without mentioning what he had done. But they also continued to be suspended above the abyss of his despair.

"And you find swamp, right?" Zoe says. "A tangled jungle of rot. I never liked the smell of that house. But maybe it was just a feeling I didn't have any other way of describing when I was a kid."

Deirdre is momentarily confused, not knowing what Zoe is talking about. She's been lost in her thoughts, which have grown darker as she notices her fatigue starting to grow at an alarming pace. Her eyes are dimming a little, her feet heavy as in one of those dreams where she's walking along a city street, but dragging her legs as through deep water. Forty-five minutes till they stop for the night. She keeps checking her watch, but time seems to have slowed down. She asks Zoe for another break, and keeps her face turned away, looking at the map, so that Zoe won't see how drained she is. When she starts to feel this way at home, Luke can always tell by the waxy pallor of her face.

They resume, and follow the trail along the edge of a cliff. Coves of unmarked sand are beneath them, cut off from human exploration by jagged headlands. Salal and huckleberry grew profusely along the trail, clouds of green in the air, giving them the illusion that they are more protected than they really are. The sun is angling, soft and golden on the rock face beside them. Soon they will need to descend the first of the long ladders to a beach to camp for the night. Although the crisis of faintness has passed, Deirdre's legs are feeling weak. Then her light-headedness returns. When they reach the ladder, Zoe goes first, scrambling down to the first platform without difficulty.

"It's fun, Mom. Going down is a lot easier than going up."

Zoe reaches the bottom and Deirdre starts the climb down, but panics once she has descended five rungs. The cliff face reminds her of how precarious she has been all winter, clinging mid-air, and the weight on her back throws off her awareness of her own strength. She has to look below her to catch each rung with her foot, but all she sees is the vast distance there, how far she could fall. Vertigo begins its slow turning in her head and she leans against the ladder to steady herself. But someone is waiting at the top to come down.

She looks down again and sees Zoe's face turned up towards her, worried, framed by her dark hair.

"Let the weight carry you down. Just let yourself go," she yells up.

Her daughter calls her down, step by step, and she obeys. It feels like the inner voice she yielded to in order to have Zoe, and then Lily. A calling, a longing, almost a homesickness deep in her body. After they lost Lily, Luke wanted to try again, but she couldn't, and soon after came her first illness and the medications she would never be free of.

The two of them prepare their camp on the beach, quietly, contrasting with the others around them who are jubilant from either their first day on the trail, or their last night before a hot bath. She can see that Zoe is preoccupied, withdrawn, and she knows that she is filled with doubts about Deirdre's strength. She's rehearsed this trail a hundred times in her mind and knows what's up ahead. There will be a canyon as deep as a skyscraper to climb down and then up on ladders bolted onto rock. There will be mudholes and slippery crossings on countless logs and long torturous climbs over rocks and tangled roots. She can't reassure Zoe because she has the same doubts.

By the next morning, she feels better, gets up before Zoe, lowering the food bag from the tree where they tied it the night before to keep it safe from cougars and bears. Most of the other hikers are gone, packed up before dawn. The sound of the waves has allowed them to sleep unaware of activity around them.

When Zoe crawls out of the tent, she says, "I had a great sleep. How about you?" This question had a casual tone, but Deirdre can hear the uneasiness. Even though she feels stronger this morning, Deirdre hasn't slept well, had endless draining dreams. The one she can remember best is of standing on the top of a tall office tower and being urged to jump to the next tower, with noisy traffic passing by below. Her shoulders are stiff and sore and she can't tell if it is from the dreams or the weight of her pack the day before.

"I slept like the dead," she says before realizing how true this is. Her dead do not rest easily.

"That's good, because this will be the day the big ladders start."

They walk along a beach with loose-packed sand. Each step is pushed deeper by the packs on their backs. They stop to photograph the twisted rusted hull of an old shipwreck. Years of winter storms have shaped the metal into a fanciful rust-coloured curl, lifting up into the sky like frozen ribbon. One can't even recognize that it was once a ship.

"The map says this particular shipwreck is from the 1920s. I wonder when it will disintegrate completely," Zoe says.

"*The centre cannot hold. Mere anarchy is loosed upon the world. Surely some revelation is at hand.*"

Zoe interrupts, "*Surely the second coming is at hand.* Yes, Mom, I know that poem inside out. My bedtime story." She laughs.

"You loved Yeats. You always asked for that poem," Deirdre says.

"Oh, the hazards of having an English teacher for a mother. Here's one for you, for right here, right now. *I must lie down where all the ladders start.*"

"Well, I hope not, because we're only halfway there. But can you finish it?"

"Sure I can. *In the foul rag and bone shop of the heart.*"

Deirdre doesn't answer. They both think quietly as they head towards orange buoys hanging at the entrance of the forest trail, then turn into the humid lush forest.

"Do you know why he did it?" Zoe asks.

"Yes and no."

"Did he leave a note?"

"I heard something about that. My mother must have read it, but I doubt she kept it."

"So you don't know why."

But Deirdre does know why and knows that whatever the note said, it wouldn't have held the key to any reason. There is no reason at that point. During the fleeting highs of his illness, everything was possible, but the lows of his manic depression were more hopeless than anything she'd ever experienced. The lows lasted a long time until something had to happen to break them.

"I see it now as a failure of love. His love for us. But also his failure to be able to receive love from anyone else. He used to get this look on his face when we were at a restaurant. He'd be watching the people at some other table laughing, having fun, and he would look so sad. He was just a lost soul."

BY THE BEGINNING of the fourth day, Deirdre is used to the ladders. She finds her pace, and is able to respond to the beauty of the trail as they move south, weaving in and out of rainforest, dodging around surge channels once the tide had receded enough for them to attempt crossings. The first cable car over a river is a funhouse slide towards the centre of the river. They are swinging in the wind, laughing and looking down at the green water rushing over stones when they realize that the tide has been going out all day and they easily could have waded across. Every time they start to pull themselves clumsily, hand over hand, to the other side, they slip back towards the middle again and laugh too hard to try again for a couple of minutes.

They slide back three times and Zoe says, "I wonder how often they've had to rescue people who are stuck on this trail because they're laughing too hard?"

Eventually, they figure out that if they put on their thin gloves and stand together, synchronizing their movements, they can jerk across to the other platform.

After climbing down through the rainforest, they emerge into strong light. The beach stretches out ahead of them, framed perfectly by the stone arch that marks the halfway point of the trail. They stop in the shade of the arch, pause to smell the wet exhalation of rock and inhale the brief silence before they cross into hot sun and waves and the tumult of gulls in the wind.

"What about you, Mom."

"What about me?"

Zoe is turned half away and asks, "Would you do that?"

Maybe Zoe has been waiting all the years since she was three years old to formulate this question. The answer has to be perfectly honest and Deirdre chooses her words carefully.

"I've never felt that alone, although I've had glimpses of what that could have been like. But only glimpses. I've been lucky. I've always wanted to be with you and Dad, to be alive."

She thinks of Luke and the way he carries more when she can't. "Your Dad makes a big difference. He's strong, and I borrow from him when I have to."

"I know what you mean. I think all those great flying dreams I have are from how he used to carry me up the stairs to bed every night when I was little."

"And he's always been able to make me laugh," Deirdre says.

"Sometimes in the morning, I would lie in bed just listening to the two of you laugh in the kitchen. It was so cozy."

Leaving the headland behind, they find the trail marker, colourfully painted buoys hung in the branches, and start the climb up to the swamp, the muddiest section of the trail. Carefully at first, they ease around each mudhole, balancing on exposed roots and inching along, but it is exhausting to balance and lean with such weight on their backs. The cedars around them are stunted, casting no shade. Whenever they encounter hikers travelling in the other direction, the weather is the topic of conversation. How incredible this sunshine is, how lucky they all are, but Deirdre is finding the sun too intense, too hot.

Over the course of the afternoon, her light-headedness returns, along with the sense that everything is unreal. She stumbles and falls. After that, she stops trying to avoid the worst of it. Zoe is still balancing like a dancer on the exposed roots, clinging to the trunks of trees and easing carefully forward to keep her boots clean, but Deirdre plods right into the middle of each hole and drags her feet through the heavy shin-high mud. Every so often an eagle circles overhead looking down on the two of them struggling through land that has suddenly become ugly. Deirdre sits down on a root without warning.

"Mom, are you okay?"

"Just a little overheated."

Zoe puts her hand on her mother's forehead, unties her bandana, moistens it with drinking water and ties it around her forehead. "You look really pale, but you feel hot."

"Don't waste the drinking water," Deirdre protests. "This is the day we don't cross a stream."

"It's not a waste if you're about to have heatstroke."

After a rest, Zoe puts on her own pack, then picks up her mother's and slips her arms through it so that it rests on her chest. Her legs look as thin as twigs, holding up the weight of both. They travel through the rest of the swamp like this, both of them now covered with mud. Deirdre keeps her eyes focused on Zoe's back, one reference point to ease her vertigo. They reach the ladders of Cullite Canyon. Deirdre sits at the base of the first ladder, and is ashamed to find herself crying. Zoe has gone ahead, but she can't summon up the courage to even try. She will never leave this spot, and it won't matter. The forest will absorb her, the way a decaying log becomes a nursery for new trees. After a while, the only sign that the older tree was ever there is the eerie alignment of new trees in the chaos of the forest.

Then Zoe is at her side, saying, "It's okay, Mom. It's okay. I didn't realize how hard this would be for you. You've been sick. Just follow me and it will be all right."

She has taken her own pack to the other side of the canyon and has returned to carry her mother's up and down the ladders. So she follows, looking only at Zoe's muddy boots, as they move rung by rung upwards and then at the top of Zoe's head as they move down a succession of steep ladders. Although she isn't wearing her pack, she feels heavy with the effort of moving her body through time and space, and is confused, seeing her backpack ahead of her, as though she is following herself. Her father must have felt this confusion, exhaustion, as well as encroaching indifference. The same indifference she felt for the first time in late winter. It wasn't the sense she experienced when her illness first emerged years ago, that she was small and everything else was too large, too vibrant to bear, but almost the opposite. That she was the only thing that continued to exist. The world receded, everyone she loved shrank to nothing, nature was obliterated, and all that was left were her own thoughts, her own tedious self. She would have done anything to escape.

But here is her daughter just a few steps ahead, now leading her across a narrow suspension bridge, only wide enough for their feet, the walls hemming them in with webs of rope. Her head is still spinning, she can't even comprehend the gorge beneath them although the rushing water of the river far below competes with the white noise in her head. Zoe stops and reaches back when they are in the centre, touching her hand on the railing made of knotted rope.

"Ignore the way we're swaying," Zoe says. "We're safe. Just concentrate on my feet."

Without answering, she does, focusing on Zoe's feet, one, then the other, moving with certainty. She can't raise her eyes and take in the spectacular drop of the canyon wall with hardy fern growing from the stone, the rainbow lifted into the air by river spray. The part of her that is curious wonders if she will regret missing out on one of the most famous features of the trail, yet she is grateful for the minute detail of her daughter's boots that allows her to cross unharmed.

The heat breaks after Zoe sets up the tent at the next cove. Zoe sleeps once the sleeping bags are unrolled, exhausted from her long haul of two packs through the swamp and up and down the canyon wall. Not to mention the ordeal of dragging her mother behind her, Deirdre thinks. The wind rises and ripples the tent, playing light across Zoe's face. She lies on her side and watches Zoe sleep, amazed at her beauty, the unlined freshness of her skin, the rejuvenation of sleep without dreams. They lie like this for at least an hour. Then the strong wind blows another weather system in from the west and suddenly it is cooler and the wind dies. Deirdre feels her strength return and soon crawls out of the tent to find the sun already dissolved in mist. The tide is low and she walks out onto the rock shelf. Everything is covered with a soft emerald fur, slippery beneath her feet. She doesn't need to squint. Everything is clear and sharply focused.

The rock is scooped out here and there with deep round tidal pools, every inch covered with life. The colours in the still water vibrate with intensity, lime-green of the anemones, old-blood hue of the starfish with its stitched sequins of outer bones, bubble-gum-pink coralline algae, blue-shelled mussels lined up shoulder to shoulder. She laughs to herself, wondering if mussels even had shoulders. Goose barnacles, white as bone, and the prickly purple sea urchin warding off touch in the crowded little world it shares with all the others. The only movements in the water are small fish darting so quickly that they almost seem like tricks of the mind.

She sees Zoe approaching her on the rock shelf, and yells, "Watch your feet. The algae is really slippery."

Zoe doesn't slow her pace. When she is beside her, she says, "Always the mother."

"I need to redeem myself."

"No, you don't, Mom. You're brave. I never realized how brave till today."

"Why? Because I sat down in the mud and cried?"

"Because you're here. No matter what, you're here. But we don't have to go on. We're close to the river crossing. We could talk to the man who runs the ferry and arrange a water taxi out to the road."

"But I love this. I love being here with you."

"We could get a pedicure in Victoria, scrape these calluses off our feet. You don't need to prove anything."

"I want to go on. I want to see what's up ahead."

Zoe smiles at her, understanding what she is really saying to her. Then she looks away, notices the deep tidal pool and says, "Oh."

"It's amazing, isn't it?" Deirdre says.

"Oh yes. The water is so still. I'm glad we got here when the tide was out. We would have missed this." She squats beside Deirdre and touches her finger to the cold surface of the water. "They are just suspended there, like souls waiting to be born."

"Or reborn."

"Yes. Or reborn." They don't need to say who they are thinking about. The tide will come in after the sun has set and all this beauty will still be here, hidden.

Bliss

S HE'S ASKED FOR FLOWERS BRAIDED into her hair. Months ago, when Deirdre was still at home, she stopped colouring it and now the grey roots are growing in. Her short French braids are a wild mixture of silver and white and faded honey brown, with the ends sticking out from the friction of the sheets. The hairdresser that comes to the hospice every week has pinned the flowers among the braids, mostly rose-coloured, bleeding to white and rimmed in sky blue. They are not real flowers but are cheap, like leis bought at dollar stores.

"Didn't you once have a fake bra covered with those flowers?" Luke asks her. "For your 50th birthday party?"

She laughs. "I should wear that bra now."

For a moment they are bantering the way they've been able to through the best of their marriage and he forgets, just as he used to forget her other spells of pain and difficulty throughout their life together. It was her gallows humour that appealed to him from the very beginning, before he knew how brave this quality truly was in her.

Deirdre smiles back at him, too wide on her fleshless face. The teeth are still very white. Her eyes are only half-open so that it looks as though she is leering. A wave of bitter grief overtakes him.

"You could," Luke says. She's reminded him of her breasts, the right one swollen and lopsided with the cancer that she allowed to grow unchecked, the left just beginning to swell. Her sternum seems to be rising from her chest like the bony head of a prehistoric whale sweeping just below the surface. Although he's not proud of it, he has to leave the room when the nurses wash her.

"There's more of me. You should be happy."

"Happy? You think this is a reason to be happy?" And he's ashamed again. He's disrupted the only normal thing left between them.

Deirdre doesn't have the energy to answer. He can see how tired she is as she shuts her eyes and says so softly he almost can't hear her, "I'm happy. Just let me be happy."

He gets out of the chair and leaves the room, knowing even as he does, that it is a meaningless gesture. She is the one leaving.

Walking down the hallway of the hospice, he can see the thin legs of other patients covered by handmade quilts, then just a glimpse of their sleeping bald heads. She should be bald too, instead of sporting that outrageous hairdo of braids and cloth flowers. He resents the fact of her hair. He can't help hating the way it's all woven together like children's daisy chains, colourful flowers riding the wave right to the edge. Not drowned like Ophelia, but partyish, like a hairdo done up for a lark. She shouldn't have hair. She should be bald like the other skeletons lying on their death beds. They could have had more time together but she threw that chance away.

SHE WINCES WHEN she wakes up, searching with her eyes for something, then relaxing a little when she sees him back in his chair.

"This reminds me of when Zoe was born," she says. "You sitting there so stable in the dark. I loved waking up to you."

"Yes, it was wonderful," Luke says. "Holding her and watching you sleep. You made the most perfect baby, I was in awe of you. It felt just as wonderful when Lily was born."

Her face becomes a little pinched, she retreats, and he sees how fragile her scaffolding has always been. He wonders if he noticed that enough through the years. He has to ask, "Did I support you enough?"

"You couldn't be here as much when Lily was born because of Zoe. I was so lost when you weren't here. And the pain that time, after the C-section. My breasts were so sore and I felt lost without you there. The nights were long. All night, motorcycles raced up and down Avenue Road."

"You know that's not what I mean," Luke says.

"She seems very alive to me. I feel her here, at night when you're not here. I never would have guessed Lily would turn out to comfort me."

"So I guess I didn't," he says.

"You didn't what?" she asks.

"Support you enough."

"Oh, you did, you did. The human condition. That's all."

This had been their code phrase whenever anything difficult or unpleasant happened and often they found a way to laugh as they said it. "Zoe threw up in the backseat." "Oh, the human condition," she would say. The climbing rose lost to winter kill, two weeks without sunlight, and darker things too, a mosque stormed by armed troops, groundswell of a new pandemic, her father's body poisoned on the garage floor. Her own long periods locked away in sadness and anxiety. The human condition.

He watches the clouds pass across her face and wonders at her. What a mystery she is, even after all these years. The memory of the happy time of Zoe's birth so much more haunting than Lily's death or what she is going through now in this hospice.

"Doesn't this hurt more?" he can't help asking.

She just smiles at him, and says, "I love you."

NOW SHE CAN'T GET ENOUGH of touch. His touch, or the nurses rubbing talcum powder onto her bony back after they sponge-bathe her. She reaches out her hand to him, the rings he placed there years ago sliding backwards so that the sapphire setting cuts into his palm.

She moans with pleasure and he's surprised that in this time and place he should be revisited by those distant voices. The anti-depressants dulled her sexuality even as they failed to heal her emotions. But she was afraid to stop taking them. He remembers lying beside her on the bed, when lovemaking had failed and turned into talking.

"I feel like I'm walking out on a glass floor," she said. "Like that glass floor at the top of the CN Tower. I could plummet, but I don't because there is this thin transparent layer. Still, I inch along, and it takes such effort, but I know the alternative."

He held her, sad for her, but also a little frustrated.

"Is it worth it? This life where you inch along?"

Deirdre didn't answer, not then. Maybe she answered that question much later, in a way he could never have predicted. Maybe he should have waited longer for her to answer, without filling the silence with his reassurance.

"You're not your father. He was always out of control."

"And plummeting. Don't forget plummeting."

Her father finally succeeded in killing himself soon after this conversation and he thought she might be set free because the worst had happened, as they always knew it would. But she remained haunted and frightened. And devastated by her own suffering through a long winter, maybe even more devastated than she was after Lily died so quietly, so mysteriously.

SHE'S ASKED FOR THE BEST sandalwood essential oil, from a small city in India. The dusty sweet smell lifts from a small clay lamp lit by a tea light candle. Before he leaves at night, he replaces the candle, and she tells him it lasts until the sky just starts to lighten.

Her hair and her gown smell like sandalwood. Even her breath seems to smell sweet. The scent is so rich and relaxed that it cancels out the smell of flowers from bouquets around the room. Even the lilies are washed out.

"You never told me before that you like sandalwood. Or did you?" Luke asks.

"I think of the water buffalo sandals I bought for $2.98 at Orientique. That whole store smelled like sandalwood. It makes me think of my long hair and thin hips and being 19."

"That was before my time," he says, suddenly acutely aware of losing her. There was a time in his life when he didn't know her and that time would come again soon.

"But whenever they come in to turn me in the middle of the night, I see the little candle and think of you lighting it for me. You're here beside me and I'm so grateful. I'm just so happy I married you."

He is sitting beside a bouquet of flowers, pink carnations piercing a damp block of green Styrofoam, dwarfed by swooping white lilies dropping their yellow pollen on his shoulder. Being so close to the lilies, their perfume snakes down his throat, irritating his lungs and making him cough. He gets up and goes into the bathroom to cup water in his hands to drink. The bright florescent light is too stark after the candlelit dimness of the bedside. There are the bright pink mouth swabs on sucker sticks, the pile of diapers, the bed pads folded neatly on the shelf. Impossible to ignore.

He moves back to her bedside to confront her. Later, when he understands better, he will regret his words.

"Dying was unnecessary. I know it and you know it."

"Please," Deirdre says weakly.

"For God's sake, can't you just tell me why?"

She watches him with a look on her face that is something like pity, but then he realizes that it is really the gaze of love when it's new and wide open. He wonders if she has hit the button on her morphine pump surreptitiously. She's half-smiling at him with such kind regard, her skin surprisingly rosy by the light turned down to almost nothing and the calm flickering of the candle.

He wants a reaction from her.

"So you prefer morphine to cancer treatment. Your father's death was just a faster form of suicide."

Deirdre closes her eyes. He's hurt her and he's immediately sorry and sits beside her again, holding her hand until her breathing tells him she's slipped back into sleep.

THE NEXT MORNING, she asks him to turn off the air conditioning unit in her window although she's hot to his touch. She tells him she likes to hear the way the day progresses out in the hospice's garden. It's June and the robins are ecstatic before dawn. Then the more moderate songbirds begin, chirping as they go about their foraging, along with the sounds of the city waking up. The metal clang of trucks pulling compartments open and closed, the soft roar of traffic blocks away. Then the sprinklers, a sound both dry and wet, like grasshoppers all leaping in unison forward, then back, then forward. The wind rising as the heat of the day builds, shaking all the birch and maple leaves, hollow cough of a basketball on pavement. Children in the garden playing while the adults visit a patient in one of the neighbouring rooms. In the afternoon, she hears the first cicada of the summer, she reaches for his hand and tries to describe it.

"A deep electric current. You feel it more than hear it," she says. "When I was little, I thought that was God and Satan fighting it out in the trees."

"Who won?" Luke asks her and she smiles, lacking the energy now to laugh.

"The Holy Ghost."

"Well, the ghost always wins. The human condition."

They hold each other's gaze, in sync, and he starts to understand how time can slow down during perfect moments.

When Deirdre's sleeping, he walks the hallways. The nurse tells him that hearing is the last sense to go. Senses close down one by one. It's ominous, the way she describes to him the things she's heard, as though the other senses are dimming.

Later she wakes up and tells him she heard her father's voice out in the garden. He was talking about fishing lines and lures, teaching Zoe how to cast out in the river, beyond the reeds at the end of the garden.

"It was nice. He was being a grandfather. Encouraging Zoe. 'Just reel it in and try again. Like this.' So patient. He never really had a chance to be a grandfather to her and I'm sad for him."

"Did he do that for you and your brother when you were children?"

"No. There was always his illness buffeting us this way and that. Always this terrible thing hanging over us. I think he was too ashamed after that first suicide attempt to look us in the eye."

"Well, you managed. You taught Zoe how to knit, how to ride a bicycle. He should have tried a little harder." There it is again—his anger with no place to go. She looks away from him and says, "Poor sad soul. He lost everything."

ANOTHER DAY, and he leans close to her ear.

"Zoe is coming in from Vancouver on the weekend," he tells her, hoping that expectation will bring her back into the room.

"Oh, she doesn't need to. She has a life of her own," she says.

"She wants to be here. You're her mother." He catches the pleading in his voice, the old habit, and lets it go. "Zoe wants to be here."

"She's away. That's good," she says. "I don't want her to worry about me." She starts to doze again.

He remembers Zoe as a newborn, and one night he almost inter-
rupted a scene of such tenderness, he'd turned quietly and went
back to bed before she noticed. She was breastfeeding in the dark
and he heard the soft vocalizing of Zoe, the uh, uh, uh, of a newborn as she drank, intertwined with a mother's cooing, a soft wordless hymn of love and comfort. He should have realized all these
years that nothing was more powerful than her desire to protect.

FIRST, SHE CAN'T BE TEMPTED by the soft furred flesh of a raspberry.
Then the gentlest of cheese, warmed to the temperature of the
body. The meats are long gone, then the vegetables. All the fruits,
one by one, are given up. Sips of ginger ale, then of water, lose all
importance to her.

He dips the pink swab in water and places it on her tongue. It
smells of mint and slips like glycerin between her dry lips. Each
time he does this, she is able to speak again. Just a word, the only
word he needs to hear now. Their love has come full circle, surrounding them and cutting them off from their grown child, ,who
sits in a plastic chair close to the foot of the bed. Zoe comes and
goes, as Deirdre has wanted her to…He can't imagine he's ever
been angry with her.

Luke speaks softly into Deirdre's ear so that these words are for
the two of them only.

"I know now. There are worse things that can happen than
this," he says, his hand gently touching her shoulder.

"Yes."

"You're safe."

"Yes."

"Home free."

"Almost."

Bare Bones

"THIS IS NOT ABOUT REVENGE," Helen says. "But I've denied myself all these years, and for what?" She's sitting on their bed, wrapped in a towel that has dried except for the chill held in the damp knot above her breasts.

It's a rhetorical question he can't possibly answer. He waits. Their future together teeters on a thin edge. He thinks of Ephram's metronome. The further the silver weight is from the centre, the wider, more voluptuous the charged quiet between ticks. A sharp sound, metal on metal, like a bullet locking into the breach.

"I never denied you. I never froze you out," he says. "You're hardly a virgin."

She ignores this and goes on as though he hasn't said a thing.

"I don't want to hurt you, Donny," she says in a reasonable tone, but she doesn't turn to meet his eyes. Gone is the uncertainty that he thought he could count on. The intimate use of his name reminds him just how personal this is. "But I was too young when I married you."

He exhales. All-out war ahead. She'll be sneaky about it, a guerrilla slipping out on her forays. Seizing the high ground even as she's down grovelling on her belly.

Then she says, "Don't worry. I won't tell you when it happens. It really has nothing to do with you. It's all about *Me, Me, Me.*"

This is a sour echo of what he told her when she overheard him on the telephone. He must have wanted her to find out, he thinks now. He had felt a terrible fatigue as he listened to the woman's voice on the phone, her secretive and needy voice. He always thought of her as the woman, even after he knew her name, Sandi, with an *i* she insisted, because he wanted to maintain the illusion that drew him to her, waifish, with her long blond hair straggling down to skinny points below her shoulder blades. She told him once that she never cut her hair, it just broke off and was shortening by the year. He first saw her browsing through strangely shaped literary magazines with stiff bright covers at the large newsstand on Rideau Street.

Helen came into the room, where he was sitting on the bed, dumped a load of laundry beside him and started folding. He was watching Helen, but the disconnect was too great, so he looked away. The woman on the phone picked up on some change, could tell even over the phone line that he wasn't paying attention.

"I can hear your computer keys," she said. "You're answering your emails, aren't you?"

"Not even close. I'm in the bedroom," he said, regretting it right away. She had never seen his bedroom, or even the inside of his house. They had always met at her house while her children were at school. He had already seen her that afternoon. She had read him her poetry. Her voice rose and fell in a rhythmic unmusical way, and it seemed to him that she was trying to manufacture passion where none existed. He was vaguely disappointed and suddenly tired.

"Why do you torment me?" she said. This was the interpretation she had settled on over the last little while. That she would never get enough of him. She was pale and insubstantial, as though she ate nothing except things that sprouted in the dark.

And he had felt powerful, with his red blood beating inside of her. But it was true. He had been impatient with the wheedling tone of her voice.

"Torment is your territory, not mine," he said, as Helen stopped folding.

Later, he refused to discuss the details with Helen. The fact of it was enough and in a way he was glad things were out and over with. The woman had taken it better than Helen had. He did it by telephone, careful that Helen wasn't in the house. The woman said she hadn't expected anything else from him; he was a man after all. He suspected there would be poems for the next man to hear.

"Just what made her so irresistible?" Helen had asked. "Is she beautiful? Did you even think of me when you were with her?"

He refused to answer, having chosen the bare bones of his script and sticking to it. He expected tears, followed by a period of cool grief, then a return to their life together, but with more tender attention paid to one another. He hadn't expected this, this tight way of keeping her emotions in check.

HE GETS UP and returns to the kitchen. He turns the burner back on beneath the pasta sauce he turned off when she came home from work, thinking that now, after a day apart, they would be able to talk about it. But he was wrong.

When she comes into the kitchen, she has nothing more to say. They look at each other blankly. Ephram is playing his violin in his room, something florid, intense and romantic—Corelli, for his upcoming exam. He knows one of them should be in there with him, counting out the beats. Their son's timing is not impeccable and he gets flustered. Normally Helen would be sitting on his bed, speeding him up, slowing him down.

The pasta sauce is now bubbling on the stove, steaming up the kitchen window. This was the best he could come up with for this evening's penance, a warm spicy smell and their glasses of red wine that stand on the counter untouched.

"He sounds better tonight," she says.

"Every day around here is like an expensive Italian restaurant," he says, hoping she will laugh, as she would have as recently as last week.

Instead, she exhales in a clipped way and asks, "You're thinking romance?"

She returns to the thought he had hoped, futilely, that she had forgotten.

"It's not romance I'm looking for," she says. "Only men are stupid enough to think they'll find romance at this age."

"Maybe I'm not finished with romance," he says. "Maybe that's the problem."

"So this is my fault?" Helen looks at him. She's furious and he doesn't want to rile her any more than he has.

"What are you looking for then?" he asks. He's frustrated that the wine and the smell of garlic, rosemary, thyme hasn't chased away the bad blood between them. "Do you want to be married or not?" he says, but he hates listening to himself, the blustering puffed-up male, the cuckold-to-be.

"That's quite the statement coming from you," Helen says. She turns towards the window, clears a small porthole with her hand to look out at the dark tangled branches of the apple tree growing close to the house. In spring, this tree offers handfuls of pink blossoms and in fall, armfuls of small inedible apples, as they sit at the table to eat. Her reflection is distorted, with condensation from the heated kitchen running down her face, as though she really is crying, but she's steely.

"Helen, don't do this."

"I need to. It's the only way for me. I'm sorry," she says, turning back towards him, leaning against the counter.

"I want to," she says finally, backing away from him, spilling her wine with her elbow. The deep red stain spreads along her side, ruining forever the pale blue of her blouse. She starts to unbutton even before she reaches the kitchen door. The glimpse of the fullness of her breasts pushed up by her bra on her thin breastbone makes him want to follow, but he knows better. He lets her go.

Only much later, still asleep in the dark stretch of predawn when she's restless and troubled in her sleep, is he aware of her breast under his hand, her gown lifted. He moves over her as she sleeps and the way she opens her legs is not submission. Her body is hard and wily under him, hungry. She opens her mouth wide against his teeth and there is a fierce click of bone on bone.

THE NEXT DAY, he comes upstairs from his office on the main floor of the house to watch her pin up her hair. When she was young, she was a strawberry blonde, but now she tames a thick lion's mane of vivid red, honey gold and startling silver into a complicated weave of a braid, ending with a tiny tail that brushes the back of her neck. This tiny tail is tucked under and pinned up as though she's hiding her animal nature beneath this demure, competent exterior. When he first met her, he loved lying on the bed watching her undergo her transformations from his untamed lover into a nurse. He can't remember the last time he watched her do this.

She still has very little to say to him. He might as well not be here. She draws on light stockings and from the back of the closet a white dress that grazes her knees. Usually she wears pants to work. He wonders if this virginal costume is a rebuke for last night's moment of weakness. The uniform makes an unpleasant raspy, almost squeaky sound when she lifts her arms above her shoulders to fasten her hair. The little knobs of her kneecaps look vulnerable in their pale stockings. She's taken off her wedding ring, as she does before every shift.

He offers to drive her to the hospital, but she says she wants to walk and get some fresh air.

"I'm not sure when I'll be done. I'll take a cab home," she says as she opens the front door. A gust of cold wind blows some dead leaves onto the white ceramic tile.

"Wait," Donny says and goes to the closet, drawing out a wool tartan scarf, his family tartan, Anderson, navy blue, green and a thin line of red, wrapping it around her throat.

Pulling it a little tighter, just enough so that she will barely feel the constriction, he says in his most intimate voice, "Hurry home." She ignores him.

He imagines she's now somewhere on the asphalt path that leads from their neighbourhood, crosses the power line, and moves through a thin band of trees before opening out to the hospital parking lot. They call it the rape path, a half-joking name based on the evidence of crimes already committed, although they've never heard of an incident. All along the length of it are high light standards with blazing bluish-tinged bulbs focused down on the winding path, making the darkness at night beyond the wide arc of light even more sinister. Bright orange signs are affixed to the poles depicting a large eye and a camera. Perhaps the signs alone are enough to discourage men from lurking around waiting for the female medical students and nurses who walk to and from shifts at odd hours.

He holds her wedding ring in his hand and imagines her at work bending over a bed, the warm scent of her underarms wafting across the face of an elderly man, emaciated, a collection of sharp bones, yellow against the white sheets. The man moans slightly and she asks him, "Are you in pain?"

She's neglected to pull the flesh-coloured curtains around his bed and the backs of her thighs are visible from the hallway. A man is passing by carrying cheap bright flowers. Although he knows where he's going, the man stops, looks at the backs of her legs, and the conversation proceeds the way these things do, starting with facts. Perhaps questions about a room number. But the stranger watches her carefully. Normally, she's a bit pale, but her cheeks have colour from her exertions over the old man. He sees her as he did years ago, drawing that long sado-masochistic hairpin out of her stiff cardboard hat although nurses haven't worn those hats for years. He sees her put her hand first on the man's shoulder, and then as his eyes grow slightly hazy, on his face.

The man has a sharp jaw she feels she must touch. His eyes are a little too close together, his Adam's apple bobs in his throat. She knows a place, hidden away and dark, in the endless light of the hospital corridors. "Wait," she whispers, as the man slips his hands over her hips. He reaches up under her skirt and discovers that her demure stocking ends in a band of lace high on her thigh.

"Wait," she says again, but she doesn't mean it. She's ready to minister to the sick and the lonely, to spread herself around. Of course it's absurd. Only in bad porn flicks do working women respond to every passing flirtation. She wouldn't wear such ridiculous stockings to work.

He's glad to be startled out of this reverie by a noise at the side of the house and moves towards the living room window, carrying Helen's rings, hot in his hands. The oil truck has pulled across the driveway and he sees a long, thick hose snaking towards the house, vanishing from sight. The clang he heard was the sound of the nozzle slipping into position. The house is sucking up the oil, the air is charged with it, an unhealthy waft of fossil fuel rises through the registers. The driver appears from the side of the house, turns with a broad smile towards the window where he's standing, and waves. How easy it would be for her. He pulls back without waving, letting the curtain fall. The hose is wound back into the truck, the length of it looks spent and victorious, drags noisily along the driveway, leaving a little smear of oil.

TONIGHT, HELEN ARRIVES back after supper. Ephram hears the front door and starts to wind his slow way from his room to the front hall, following along behind her playing the Corelli again on his violin.

"Hello, my favourite son," she says to Ephram, bending slightly to kiss him on the cheek.

Ephram loses just one beat to answer, "Only son."

This is their standard greeting and Ephram's fingers scuttle like fast spiders on the strings, his arm moving the bow more passionately now that she's home to hear. A wave of sound follows her, like a too-loud movie score. He approaches to kiss his wife on the cheek but takes one of Ephram's quickly moving bow strokes in the gut before he can reach her. She laughs.

"What's so funny?"

"Nothing," she says.

"You like seeing me hurt?" he asks. Ephram continues to weave between them.

"Practice in your room! Leave your mother alone," he yells. Silence drops over the three of them suddenly as Ephram lowers his violin to his side and looks away, towards the floor, ashamed that he has been noticed following his mother around like a sissy.

"I decide if it's enough. You hear me?" Helen says.

Helen glares at him, then breaks the standoff by turning to Ephram, lifting his chin and saying, "Hi, sweetheart. You sound fantastic. How was your day?"

Donny sees that Ephram is happy to be given this chance to hide his hurt feelings, but he casts a wary glance at his father.

"Guess what caused the ice age?" he says, tucking the violin under his arm like a shield, the way he's been taught to.

"Is this a riddle?" Helen says. "Well, let me think. Somebody was in a bad mood."

"No! It's science, Mom."

"Someone couldn't bear the perfection of the planet, the lush green—all the reptiles moving slowly through the warm swamps without a care in the world." Ephram thinks she's still joking but Donny hears the bitterness.

"That's not science," Ephram says.

"Lust, selfishness, just plain nastiness are part of evolution. Where would we be without them?" This is for him.

"Mom!"

"Do you have a better idea?"

"A giant asteroid from outer space. Boom! And then the dust caused everything to get cold and dark, which killed off the dinosaurs and turned their bones into stone. And it could happen today. There are asteroids all over the place."

"Don't I know it," Helen says.

LATER, IN THEIR BEDROOM, they have sex, good for both of them. Then she says things to him that make him feel ashamed. Through the night he remembers her voice and the way it sounded both beautiful and frightening. Beautiful, with its feminine idiosyncratic lift in the middle of sentences. Frightening in her complete dismissal of him. He's agitated all night. He hears her over and over in his head. This is what she said: "Did you know that you aged twenty years in five minutes? Suddenly, there you were, a pathetic middle-aged man. No different from any other."

He lies in bed as she sleeps beside him, looking unselfconscious and contained, maybe even a bit smug. He remembers her last summer dabbing at an infected wound on his backside. He had sat on a shingle nail that had landed on a patio chair. The neighbours had just had their roof redone, and it was only after this mishap that he thought to climb up and clean out the eaves trough. He hadn't mentioned it, but she noticed the little puncture a few days later, when it had grown red and sore. After a tetanus shot she insisted on, she cleaned and changed the small gauze square twice a day.

"Tell your mistress not to be so rough," she had said and kissed, then slapped, his buttock. She seemed to be enjoying playing nurse and he had a sense of how humiliating his future would be, with her tending his body as efficiently as she handled cold poultry on the way to the oven. She had always said she would outlive him. She kissed and patted Ephram's bottom exactly that way, during diaper changes when he was a baby. And here he is, well on his way to old age, as far as she's concerned. He thinks bitterly that he's collapsed in on his own clichés, while she is someone surprising and new. Someone he hasn't laid eyes on for years. Someone who can always slip away, her body sealing over like a pool closing over a stone.

HE'S FOLLOWING HER. He's not proud of this, but there it is. He's cleared work from his calendar for her day off. It will happen soon, that he knows. His wife has never been one to procrastinate, a quality that makes her such a wonderful nurse. The way she moves inside her jeans is no-nonsense, as though she can barely wait to get out of them.

She stops to talk to Anastasia, their elderly Russian neighbour, near the grocery store. Although Anastasia shuffles along slowly, the top half of her is ever in motion, hands waving, red hair hennaed and blowing in the wind. Helen is wearing purple gloves and her hands mirror Anastasia's, fly around as she talks. The two of them look like they are conducting a symphony, all mischief and high spirits, but all he can hear from behind a blue spruce is the rattled-pod sound of the wind.

Anastasia has had four husbands. "Lucky in love," Helen has said to him, being fond of her.

"Not so lucky for the men," he answered, but she wouldn't laugh now. With how she's feeling about him, she would say Anastasia has been unlucky to have so many husbands. Now the significance of this dawns on him. So they talk about men, he realizes. He's come home from meetings and heard the two of them cackling in the kitchen over tea but never wondered what they found so funny. He's also heard Anastasia's low voice soothing, sympathetic, and Helen's, soft and indistinguishable. Has she told her about what's going on? What kind of advice was offered? As he watches them talking on the street, he can almost hear Anastasia, in her accented crone's voice, giving Helen pointers, like a madam in a whorehouse educating a new recruit.

Keep him guessing what you'll do next.

Remember, he wants you on your knees.

Find that hollow at the base of his spine and caress.

The sinewy explicit voice is irresistible. He sees Helen doing all these things to a faceless man, her wild hair, excited with static, electrifying another man's thighs. He tries to remember if he saw her wedding ring in the dish beside the sink and wills her to remove her purple glove so he can see her left hand. But she reaches out her gloved hand to Anastasia before she moves on.

He follows and waits outside the grocery store. After just fifteen minutes, she comes out with more bags than she can comfortably carry home. Moving fast along a parallel street, he's there with his coat off when she arrives. He opens the door for her, takes the bags.

"You should have taken the car. Or told me and I would have gone with you."

"Well, you know how it is," she says. "Faced with all that choice, it's so hard to tease out what you need from what you want."

"What the hell does that mean?" he asks.

She looks at him with her fine pale brows drawn together, mouth pursed. Helen is not one to blush. Her emotions are too controlled for that, but the pale skin around her eyebrows reddens when she's embarrassed or perturbed. And her eyes get a slightly bloodshot look to them, as though she's been crying, but she never sheds a tear.

"What do you think I mean?" she asks, temper flaring.

"What you want. What you need." He hates the vindictive way his voice mocks her but he can't stop it.

"You know what? This is crazy." And she's gone to the kitchen, having grabbed the bags out of his hands, tinned food hitting her legs so hard he knows they'll leave bruises on her pale skin.

HE'S HIDING ALONG the rape path, waiting for Helen to pass on her way to work. She's a little late today, which gave him the chance to get here first and scout out a hidden place. The wild lilacs and thorn bushes along the path are bare this time of year so he's been forced to retreat to the thick stunted boughs of the spruce that grow along the power line. The hydro company must have come along recently and cut the tall tops off the mature trees. The thick bottoms end abruptly in unnatural light, but he's hidden.

She was talking on the telephone when he left. When he picked up the receiver in his office he heard her voice, "You have to watch out for those tiny bones," she said. "If you're not careful, they'll stick in your throat." She laughed. Then she said, "Is that someone on your end? The connection's changed."

"No. That's on your end," a woman's voice said, someone he couldn't identify. There was silence as Helen considered this, and he hung up. Then he listened outside their bedroom door where Helen was getting ready for work as she talked on the phone to someone else.

"I was thinking of you." A pause. "Maybe not." She was speaking quietly, confidentially and he could only make out phrases here and there.

"Soon," she said, and he felt a sick turn in his stomach.

Now, waiting for her, he sees her ambling along the path. She's moving more slowly than usual, with troubled eyes looking upwards. The light illuminating her is unnaturally bright, as though she's on a movie set, and he can see her internal thoughts as though she is the most brilliant of actresses. She's clearly pale and strained, eyes ringed with tiredness. Then a flash of guilt. At least he hopes it's guilt. But all her emotions, no matter how painful, make her appear worthy of an audience's intense focus.

Then she stops walking towards him, looking at the truncated treetops just above where he's hidden and his heart starts to pound with a kick of adrenaline. But she doesn't know he's here, so close he could almost reach out and grab her. She touches the collar of her jacket and pulls it closer with a little shiver. Her face is luminous in the unfamiliar light, pale, and her hair so fiery and wild, despite the neat job she's done with pins and braiding, folding and tucking.

Then he sees the change register in her face like fleeting sadness. Sadness for the loss of the green swaying crowns of the trees or for her innocence he wouldn't know. The light doesn't penetrate to her thoughts, but she is dazzling. She walks on, passes him, and he edges out of his hiding place. Her shoes are soundless, but sexy in the way she plants each foot straight and delicate as a deer in brush. Then she's out of sight.

He's not quite free of the trees when he hears the sound of running feet. He turns and sees a woman careening away from him, also dressed in nursing clothes. Her breath is ragged with her exertion, and he can't see her face but knows from the flailing way her limbs pump hard and fast that she's terrified of him.

THIS IS HIS SIXTH COFFEE in the hospital cafeteria. Maybe it's the speedy effects of institutional caffeine, but he's growing bolder. Nurses come and go on breaks or the ends of shifts. Most of them are laughing and if he closes his eyes he could almost be back in high school. Almost, though, because back then he wouldn't have been able to take his eyes off the incredible variety of women. Young women coming out of the washroom, stray hairs rising like halos around their heads. The variety of hip bones, sharp or softly moulded, the scent of females everywhere.

But these nurses all seem pretty generic to him in their pastel uniforms and sensible shoes. It's the men who hold his attention: the muscular new breed of male nurses wearing scrubs, the orderlies with little pot-bellies and quick efficient movements, janitors pushing defeated brooms, knowing that they're the bottom of the food chain. And the doctors, always the officious, balding but ever-more-virile male doctors. Even if the women here in the cafeteria didn't keep a respectful distance, he'd know who the doctors were.

"I heard you were down here," Helen says. "What are you doing?'

She's standing just behind his left shoulder and he doesn't know how long she's been looking down at his neck or counting the coffee cups on his table. He has to turn around to see her properly. Her hands are on her hips, but then he sees that they're not. Her hands are together, demurely joined, level with her groin.

He can't think of anything to say.

"Are you spying on me," she says, but not as a question.

"What do you expect from me," he says.

"Maturity," she says.

"What's so mature about revenge?"

Now it's her turn to look at him with nothing to say.

"It's just an excuse, isn't it? There's someone, and now you have the justification to do what you want to do. And you can blame it on me," he says.

"I'm not talking to you when you're like this," she says, starting to turn away.

"Is it him?" He grabs her with one hand, pulls her back towards him, points with the other hand at one of the doctors. "Or him? That guy with the muscular thighs. I bet you'd lap that up."

"Stop it," she hisses at him.

"Or maybe that one, the dark poetic type."

She cuts him short. "Fuck off," she says.

They look at each other. He can't help but feel a little skirmish of victory in his chest when she's the one to look away.

They end up going for lunch. He doesn't care why. She came close to turning around and walking away from him, and if she had, it would have been forever. She doesn't seem surprised when he ushers her into a cab at the hospital entrance, and in his confusion about where to take her, he automatically gives the name of a restaurant he's been to several times before, *Jack's*, although not with her. Luckily, the waitress doesn't seem to remember him.

They sit at a narrow wooden table adorned with a small white bowl of sea salt, and almost standing upright in the salt, a silver spoon small enough for cocaine. There is also a thin green vase holding one long and bending sprig of tropical fern and incredibly, a woodland flower, a jack-in-the-pulpit.

"Is it real?" Helen asks, reaching out her fingers to stroke the firm green polyp that is Jack and the smooth green-and-white striped hood.

He reaches out and barely misses her hand as he touches the flower. The soft plastic is cool to the touch.

"No. But a very good fake," he says.

Like you, he can see her thinking, but she won't lower herself enough to say it out loud.

He drinks beer and she sips tea as they wait for sandwiches that will look frazzled and exotic when they arrive, garnished with some kind of sprouts he has never seen in a grocery store. They talk about Ephram's upcoming violin exam, carefully, almost formally, sharing a concern and both of them are humbled by what they have in common.

"You're awfully hard on him," she says. "He's still so little." She's almost apologetic, cautious. He thinks before answering.

"He's too hard on himself. He thinks he isn't allowed to make a mistake. I'm trying to give him some perspective."

"Oh, perspective," she says, formulates a thought, then lets it go.

A young couple sits down at the table beside them, so close that he knows these two tables are normally one table for a larger, undoubtedly more boisterous party. The young woman sits next to Helen, attractive, shoulder-length blond hair. She's wearing a tight thin-strapped top more suitable for summer. Her light brown arms are bare and covered with goosebumps. The man beside him keeps leaning forward, meeting her lips across the table. He hasn't seen the man's face, just the glossy back of his hair, curling down voluptuously over his collar. Their hands intertwine, stroking and exploring each other's fingers and palms. The kiss deepens. Then they draw back, staring deeply and quietly at one another. They draw apart whenever the waiter asks them what they would like, but wine is all they seem to want. Wine, and each other. He remembers only too well. But instead of missing the other woman, he misses Helen, even though she's sitting across from him.

He continues talking, trying to fill in the silences. Now they're talking about work. He's telling her about a start-up company that's doing well. Meanwhile, the couple moves in closer so that their feet are entwined and their legs touch. Helen tells him about a piece of equipment that went on the fritz and how much scurrying around they've had to do without it. They're being so polite, neither of them willing to acknowledge what's going on beside them.

Finally it's time to leave. The couple is still lost in their timeless explorations, wine glass still bearing the lipstick mark of her now-bare lips. He wonders if Helen didn't notice the couple after all. She hasn't given any kind of sign. But then she turns to him as she's slipping one arm into her jacket, leans towards him and says, "Nothing makes a person crazier than sex."

She shakes her head almost imperceptibly, sadly. "I don't envy them at all." Then she pauses to put her arm through the other sleeve. "Or maybe I do."

This is typical of the new Helen, leveling this at him, setting him off balance, then turning away, all innocence.

SHE'S LATE COMING HOME. Ephram is in bed, and now Donny is free to move from window to window, waiting for the headlights of a taxi to light up the formal dining room they never use. The violin exam will be the day after tomorrow and Ephram has been restless. After Ephram is finally asleep, Donny remembers that he forgot to go over the study and the scales with his son. He forgot about the monotonous part of practice, just as important as the flashy Corelli. He had been impatient with Ephram, and instead of slowing the tempo, he had insisted that a good night's sleep would be better than practice. All the while wishing for the door to open and Helen to walk back into their lives. It feels as though she's been gone for years.

From the kitchen window he watches the main road behind their house. When he sees a car's lights, he moves to the dining room to see if it is the taxi carrying her home. But for almost two hours, it is not. He keeps hearing her voice saying *Maybe I do*, like some cynical wedding vow, half-given, half-meant. Even though he thought they were getting somewhere at lunch, that maybe she wouldn't need to do what she so obviously had already planned to do. Tonight. Tonight, as he was pacing the house, trapped.

When she finally pulls into the driveway, she takes a long time to get out of the taxi. The driver is turned around and she's talking to him. The conversation goes on long enough that he expects to witness a good-night kiss. Maybe this was the guy. Maybe she's been riding taxis all night looking for some guy who would say yes, his legs hanging out the open back door, pulled over next to the river or parked with the motor running in the cemetery.

She comes through the front door with her hair disheveled, mouth pale and bare of colour. Her eyes are puffy.

"Where were you?"

She stops, looks at him.

"Are you happy now? Is that what you needed?" he says, not wanting an answer.

"I need a bath," is all she says.

"I bet you do." He's standing over her, not caring if his height is intimidating. All the courtesy is gone between them, as far as he's concerned. "I never rubbed your nose in it, not once."

She puts her hand in the centre of his chest, and he's shocked because it's a gesture he remembers from that distant long-ago time of their mutual seduction. The way she used to slip her left hand between the buttons of his shirt, pressing against his breast-bone, saying, "Do you have a heart in here?" But she pushes, steadily, until he has to step back.

"I'm tired," she says. "Leave me alone."

He lets her go, leaves her to the sound of the bath running behind closed doors. But anger lights its fuse in his chest, and he confronts her again. She's locked the door from the hallway, but not from their bedroom. Then he's standing over her, blocking the light. He's never felt so huge, with her lying below him, her hair rippling softly beneath the surface. There's a slickness to the bath water. Maybe a rank smell. He looks at her hips, scans her thighs for redness. She rises suddenly and grabs a towel from the rack beside the tub and pulls it down and over her, but not before he catches sight of her pink aureoles, punished a little darker by some other man. The towel darkens in the water.

"Give me a moment's peace," she says. "For God's sake, just leave me in peace." There's no fight in her voice. Water continues to run down her face. She sniffs, stuffily, then breaks into a sob. Her voice rises and echoes off the mirror, the ceiling. She's crouched over the soaked towel as it weaves underwater, reacting to her every sharp breath, sending shock waves through the bathwater. He can see all the bones in her back, the shoulder blades, the backs of her ribs buttoned to her vertebrae, the thin flesh over the scaffolding twitching, almost convulsing, with emotion. She rocks forward and backward, holding the towel against her breasts.

She's keening in her own private world and then it feels obscene to be standing over her so he sits down on the toilet seat. He closes his eyes for a moment. The anger is gone, replaced by a hollow sadness, just a fraction of what he sees brimming over in her. She's balancing herself with a hand on the edge of the tub, the towel having finally fallen away. He's filled with tenderness for the delicate knob he can see at the base of her neck, the hair straggling out of its pins and flattened against her skin, and then by all of her. He does the only thing he can. He moves to her, puts one hand on the back of her neck, the other on her hand. Miraculously, her hand turns and grasps his. She's gasping now.

"I never knew," he tells her. "I wouldn't have done it if I knew … " but he can't say it.

Her voice cries out again and then through force of will she slows her breathing.

"No. No, you don't get it," she says in a small voice. He doesn't want her to continue but now he knows that he hasn't any right to demand anything from her.

"As I was leaving, I saw her on a gurney in the hallway. She was alone. I knew her by the colour of her hair." She stops, turns her face towards him and he's shocked by how distorted she looks. There's a vein pulsing in her forehead, her eyes are almost swollen closed.

"What are you saying, Helen?" He's feeling disoriented.

She puts her face against his chest, almost pulls him into the water with her. First the water is warm, then quickly cool. He shivers, but she doesn't notice because now she's shaking too. Like that old superstition, someone has walked over their graves.

"She was so terrified. She begged me to stay with her."

"Who are you talking about?" he asks, panicking a little. "Did something happen at work?"

"It's not work," she says. "It's life or death. Oh, God. Oh, God."

"It's all right. It's all right," he whispers as he rocks her, holding her wet body. She feels as though she will slip out of his grasp at any time.

"No. It's not all right. She needed me. She wouldn't let go of my hand. I had to pull her fingers back, one by one."

"Who?"

"Anastasia. She was so frightened. I just went to check when a room would be ready."

"She was at the hospital?"

"She was brought in. Her heart had gone crazy. Too fast, too slow. All over the place." She pauses, tries to compose herself and says, "When I got back, she was shaking. She was arching her head back and I put my hand on her forehead. But she wasn't breathing."

"She died?" he asks, still confused.

She doesn't answer. He strokes her wet hair, kisses her temple, but it's an awkward posture he can't sustain, separated as they are by the cold low wall of the tub.

"She knew you were there," he tells her. She lets go of him, curling back over herself in the water.

"No, she didn't. It was just her nervous system shutting down. She was alone. But how could you understand that?" The first note of recrimination in that, the first hint that she's not ready to receive comfort from him.

He wants to answer, to find just the right thing to say to draw her closer to him, stop her shaking, but he sees that she needs to be alone with her grief. He thinks of the days of silence they will spend together, cut off from each other, stripped down to bare bones. And the work he will have to do to change things.

Then suddenly they are not alone. They must have disturbed Ephram's sleep. He's not with them physically in this damp miserable bathroom but he's awake down the hall in his room, starting the upward ascent of a scale. The violin plods up and down the compulsory scales he didn't practice before he went to bed. He stops and his father can only hear the faint tick of the metronome counting out the beats. Helen is breathing out of time. There's a stumble, forlorn silence, and he waits to find out if Ephram will be able to catch the right pitch again.

The Men Have Gone Hunting

LAST EVENING, SHOTS WERE FIRED in the bush around the farmhouse, although officially hunting season started this morning at dawn. They live just north of highway number 3 which runs horizontally, cutting the province of Saskatchewan in two, north from south. The season starts one week earlier in the northern half, where the forest begins, and the muskeg and the lakes that are cold even in the heat of summer. All the hunters from the cities drive just as far as this line drawn in the snow before loading their guns.

She had settled Maya in her crib for her afternoon nap when she heard the knocking on the kitchen door. Looking down on the stoop from the upstairs window in the hall, she could see the guns propped over the men's shoulders, the bright orange hunting vests hurting her eyes against the unfamiliar white. The winter snow had come only two days before and she wasn't used to it. She couldn't see a truck in the yard, not even any footprints so she couldn't tell if they'd walked in by way of the overgrown northern approach or looped around, following the towering caragana that swung closer to the barn.

She ducked, hoping Maya wouldn't wake up, but heard the knocking again. Not daring to raise her head, she squatted beneath the window ledge, hoping they would go away. Norman was further north, hunting as well, in the vast unpopulated forest reserves. He thought that only rude city folk would hunt in places where people lived. Even though he was a city boy himself. He'd taken up these opinions over the two years they had lived in rural Saskatchewan, first renting a small bungalow in Glaslyn, then a rambling farmhouse out in the country.

Last November, her first with him in the country, she'd been pulling Maya in her sled, wearing a scarlet jacket against the new snow. A truck had pulled over and the man had said to her, "You're going to get shot walking the roads this time of year. Do you want to leave that little one without a mother?" Norman was incensed when he heard what a stranger had said to her practically in her own driveway, but he couldn't be dissuaded from leaving her alone this year too. It's what the men in his family had always done, even though they were now two generations removed from rural living. He told her a little self-righteously that she would have to give up her city sensitivities if she was going to be happy here.

She heard the kitchen door opening and the men's footsteps in the mud room. Heavy steps moving into the house. A glance out the window confirmed it. The two black rifles were leaning against the door frame but the men were gone.

"Anybody there?" she called to them as she moved down the stairway, saying what they should have been calling out as they entered her house.

One of the men was rifling through the key rack near the door, the other had walked across the kitchen to the phone. The floor was wet and muddy; he hadn't taken off his boots.

They both looked up at her without surprise.

"Hey," the one at the key rack said. "We slid off the road. This snow's a bitch."

"Goddamn prairie gumbo," the other near the phone said. "The Indians can have it."

"You prick. If you'd just given them our booze, they wouldn't have run us off. Those guys are probably at the car right now, cutting the deer off the roof and stealing our beer. Goddamn land claims. Where the fuck are we anyways?"

He looked at her and smirked.

"The reserve is just north of here. Where's your car stuck?"

She wanted to make this clear because she'd sometimes been mistaken for a mixed-blood, with her long black hair and lean build. She could smell alcohol in the room, but stale so she knew they could be getting cranky as the buzz wore off.

The man by the key rack wore glasses, which made him seem more trustworthy. Maybe an ordinary guy who sat at a desk in Saskatoon, only playing at being tough one week a year. Maybe a man like her husband. She spoke to him.

"You need a phone book to call the garage in town?" And she turned away, bending to the cupboard where she kept the book, bending from the knees instead of her waist so that her backside didn't present itself to either of them.

The other one answered, the alpha, even though he was shorter, almost hunched and had dark circles under his eyes. "You've got a tractor. Where's your husband? He can pull us out."

"Out in the back forty," she answered, hoping that she made sense. They didn't farm, although they lived in a farmhouse with an empty hip-roofed horse barn, a fragrant pile of silage out behind the slough. The man they rented the house from pastured cattle there, arriving silently every morning before dawn to fire up the tractor and spread silage in the coldest, darkest months. They never saw him, probably wouldn't recognize him if they met in the Red and White store in town. She could always tell he'd been there because every morning, there was a lingering smell like rotten fruit, even on days so cold that moisture crystallised before it dissipated.

And she saw tracks in the snow where he'd driven the tractor out to the silage pile and back.

"The tractor's sitting right there. I can drive one. Which is the right key?"

Taken aback, she admitted, "I don't know."

"Can't you call him?" the one with tired eyes answered although she hadn't spoken to him.

She looked at him without comprehending.

"Your husband," he said, a little sarcastically, as though the word was just a way of putting on airs. He held his hand like a gun to his head, thumb pointing to his mouth, mocking her.

"You know, phone?" mincing on his small feet. She broke eye contact, studied the pattern in her linoleum, the water that had gathered along the indentations, one of their boot prints that had dried almost white against the red. "Doesn't he carry a cell?"

"Cell? There are no cells here. No coverage outside the city," she answered as she flipped through the slim phone book looking for the number of the garage.

"Coverage! No coverage! Don't wet your panties about it," he said.

"Hey, hey, no need for that," his friend told him. "If you could call the garage then."

When the garage didn't answer after dialling the number over and over for five minutes, she left a message and then called her neighbour, Harold, who had a woodworking business he ran from his house three kilometres away. She tried to look neutral as she listened to him berating the uselessness of hunters, clamping the phone close to her head so they wouldn't overhear.

"If they're stupid enough to ditch their car, they can hitchhike back to the city as far as I'm concerned."

"Yes, yes," she murmured, which only spurred Harold on.

"They come up here, get drunk and shoot cows in the pasture because they don't know any better and then they want to be bailed out."

"They're here in my kitchen," she said softly, almost warmly, as though she was so happy to have these unexpected visitors. "All they need is a little push, or a pull with your truck and they'll be on their way."

"I wouldn't waste one millilitre of gas on those buffoons."

"They've been sitting here, just waiting. The garage is not answering. If you could just come over, please. Norman's gone hunting up north," she said, realizing too late that she'd revealed that she was alone. And hoping she didn't sound too pleading, too desperate.

"I don't run when hunters call. Sorry," he said, and then again, more gently, "Sorry."

She could tell that he was still feeling badly about yelling at her when she had the chimney fire last winter and had placed Maya in the snow wrapped in a big comforter and gone back in to throw pails of water on the smoking wall. He was ranting about city people not knowing anything about living in the country. Hadn't they cleaned the pipes? Why was Norman always at work when these things happened, making big bucks teaching while his neighbours had to scrabble up a little work building cabinets for those cottages owned by people who sat on the best land.

AFTER TELLING THEM that her neighbour's truck was in the shop and that they should try the garage again, she left the kitchen and went down the cellar steps to put more wood in the furnace, but once she was done, she sat on the woodpile thinking of what to do next. Maybe she could stay down here and they would eventually leave. But Maya was two floors above her, sleeping lightly in her three-year-old way. A girl now, not a baby. A pretty brown-eyed girl. She wasn't in a crib anymore and might wander downstairs on her own, trailing her striped blanket behind her, if she woke up.

She heard movement upstairs. One of them was still wearing boots, probably the short one, she thought maliciously. Isn't it always the short one? She could also hear a creaking of the floor joists moving in the other direction, almost as though a ghost was up there protecting her, blocking the stairway going to the second floor. Then her heart started pounding hard. The other had obviously taken off his boots and was moving furtively. Was he about to go up the stairs? Why weren't the two of them together? She stood up, listening from the bottom of the cellar stairs. She heard drawers opening and closing in her kitchen. They were obviously looking for something. She heard a rustling sound like paper crinkling and more cupboard doors being opened and then gently closed. The two men were moving methodically around her large kitchen. She could sense one of them standing at the base of the stairs leading to her daughter's room. She took a deep breath and headed up from the cellar.

They must have heard her coming because she heard their footsteps quickly move towards one another and a secretive conversation too low for her to make out. She was sweating down her back even though the basement was cool and the woodpile conducted the temperature of the frozen ground into the house. As she reached the top of the stairs, the phone rang. One long ring, then two short ones—her ring. Even though the men wouldn't have known that, one of them answered the phone. She stood at the door of the kitchen, hoping it was the garage calling back, so they would go and wait beside their ditched car. The taller one was on the phone, while the shorter man wearing boots sat at her kitchen table. She saw a box of crackers lying open on the floor.

"Yeah, she's here," he was saying. The person on the other end was talking for a while and she thought that was strange. What could the man at the garage have to say to this stranger? Then he started describing the buck tied to the top of his car.

"Four point antlers. A real stud. Not an easy kill either. He was a smart bugger. Jumped a fence from standing and hid near a slough. Knew enough to keep that rack low in the willows."

More silence and she felt disoriented. She looked out the window, not entering the kitchen completely until she understood what was going on. Hoarfrost had grown on all the tangled branches of the caragana and now the days were too cold to burn it off by afternoon. The windbreak was once again opaque as it was in summer, impenetrable. From the road, only the side of the barn was visible. The house would be completely hidden again, after a brief bright period of sunlight in the shortening afternoons. The barn's faded red paint looked like old blood in the white light of early winter. And the rolling prairie behind the house almost blended into the sky, seeming to go on forever. She felt a bit dizzy, as though she was lost on a vast, still, white ocean. Two by two by two—they were trapped together, but there was one too many. She was the odd one out here even though it was her house.

The man was laughing. "Bugger," he said. "My buddy lost his boot in a sinkhole of mud. Smelled like hot springs. He's got a wet foot and I told him to keep his boots on. Who needs that stink?"

Then there was silence again, punctuated by laughter.

"A clean shot, my buddy thought… But it must have missed the bone, went sailing out into the air. Could that buck run. Holy fuck, I never saw anything like that, a real buck Olympics. Right over the fence."

Silence as the person on the other end talked.

"… the white flag down. A smart bugger. 'Where'd he go?' my buddy says. 'Too much beer for breakfast,' I says. Then we see him bounding across the field, making a flying leap into the willows around a slough. 'We got him,' I says, but to be safe we came from two different direction."

More silence.

"I says, 'Don't you shoot me by accident.' Watch where you aim."

A story was being told on the other end, she could tell, because the man on the phone cradled the phone on his shoulder as he scratched his neck with pleasure. He was grinning.

"How're you going to get them out of the bush?" he asked. "Better not run into the law. No law shit up there. Maybe we'll head up next weekend."

The back and forth of conversation continued.

"Hey, raise a cold one for me, buddy. I could use a bit of your luck."

"Yeah," he said. "We slid off the road. Had to move over for a big truckload of Indians. The buck on the roof should give us traction but my buddy's tires are pieces of shit. City road shit."

More silence, then he was back to telling the story of the kill.

"Yeah. I told my buddy, 'Don't just aim and fire. I'm coming in from the other side. We'll get him. All it takes is patience.' And there he was, hiding his head in the willows. Smart bugger. But we flushed him out and his head's going to look real good on my wall."

The man in the boots sitting at her table was following along even though he, too, couldn't hear the other half of the conversation. He was grinning, and even pointed his finger at the man on the phone and narrowed one eye as though he was aiming a gun when he was describing for the third time how they surrounded the buck hiding in the willows.

"Then we got him, clean. He was all worn out and fell on the spot. A clean shot. Didn't even bleed that much."

Then suddenly, the conversation was over and the man on the phone looked at her and said, "Barb?"

She was shocked. How did he know her name?

He held the phone out to her and she hesitated, then moved into the kitchen, aware of the man sitting at the kitchen table, his eyes level with her breasts.

SHE TOOK THE PHONE, trying to avoid touching the man's hand. The phone was warm against her ear, making her feel a bit queasy.

"Hello?"

"Hey, Barb. You've got some excitement there, don't you?"

"Norman! Where are you? Are these guys friends of yours?"

"No. No, Barb. Just the fellowship of hunters."

"Are you coming home?"

"No, Barb. I'm calling from a gas station. We walked half the night and spent the other half sitting in the doorway, waiting for someone to show up. When we got back to the truck last night, all the tires were flat. Someone slashed them, way out here, in the middle of nowhere. It's the strangest thing. And we had three deer— two does and a buck. Over our limit, I know, but what a day it was, until the truck. We had to hide one in the forest, under some brush. Maybe we'll get back … "

She cut this off, this story that had nothing to do with her situation right now, at that very moment.

"The garage doesn't answer here. And Harold wouldn't come. He wouldn't help."

"Harold's a jerk."

"That may be true, but I have a kitchen full of strangers with guns."

Too late she realized that they were listening to her end of the conversation. Norman seemed to know this before she did because his voice was suddenly warning, low, as though coaxing a bear to back off and let them go. That had happened once, when they were walking through the poplar forest near the community pasture. A bear came out of nowhere and he put himself in front of her and Maya, talked slowly, carefully to the bear. The bear snuffled from side to side, sending whiffs of its oily fur to her, so that it seemed to be even closer. Then it moved over to a tree, stretched to its full length and clawed the bark. She had wanted to run, but Norman continued talking gently, slowly, as though trying to hypnotise the bear to turn away.

"Listen carefully, Barb. Smile and give them some food. They're cranky with the hunting, the high of the kill, then the frustration of sliding off the road. Things can happen at a time like that. So smile and give them some coffee."

"You want me to play happy hostess?" she almost spit this at him as quietly as she could.

"Careful, Barb. Don't let them see your fear. Or your resentment."

"A little late for that."

"You can do this. You can smile as you're talking to me. You can send them the message that I'm welcoming them into my home. That I'm there even though I'm not."

She was silent now, considering, her eyes surveying the kitchen, the lump in her throat rising when she saw that they had taken in everything that she'd said. The tall one was looking down, avoiding her eyes, but the short one was sitting at her table with his boots on, legs splayed so that she could see dark bloody stains on the thighs of his jeans. He was watching her, almost sneering. His hand was resting palm up on the table, the illusion of ease. But she could feel something in him coiled tight, ready to spring. She looked away and concentrated again on Norman's voice coaxing her, cajoling, intimate in her ear.

"Smile. Pretend I'm telling you about the first doe I shot. Give them something to eat. Listen to me. Don't talk, just listen."

Persephone Without Maps

THESE ARE THE FIRST bright days of fall, when the light suddenly reaches the ground without interference—theatrical light, just right for the costumes I can see through the windows of Jonah's school bus. Excited voices seem to suddenly escalate as the bus pulls to a stop. There are bobbing witches' hats, smiling green faces, plastic scythes held high. A hand scratches the steamy glass wearing some long-nailed contraption.

Jonah starts down the steps with a big smile on his face. The gauze bandages I wrapped around him this morning, and toilet paper once we had used up all the bandages in the house, have drifted down like a spare tire around his middle. He reaches down and jacks his costume up further on his hips so his legs can reach the distance from the last step to the ground. He shakes the jack-o-lantern wand at me, the one he insisted a mummy must have in its hand. I'm impressed he has managed to hang onto it through the excitement of touring the school, class by class, parties and games. I'm delighted the makeshift mummy costume has fared as well as it has.

"My teacher gave me candy," he says, rooting down into the depths of his shredding costume. I see that he's unravelling, dragging yards of tattered toilet paper and gauze behind him as he walks, a little grotesque bride. He finds what he's looking for and shows me candy in the shape of fangs.

"My goodness. Do you eat those or do they eat you?"

He pierces the fangs with his own teeth and discovers that they can stay attached that way, pushing against his lower lip with their fake dripping blood, although I don't understand another word he says. I catch something about the costumes he's seen today: dragons and princesses, skeletons, and he takes the fangs out to tell me about the one he liked best.

"Her eyes were in the centre of the painting, and they moved, just like a painting in a scary house."

"What was the painting?"

"It's famous. Moaning Lisa."

I smiled down at him.

Every so often, a short length of toilet paper breaks off the train behind him and is swept away by the wind. We hear the high hysterical laughter of older girls far behind us. I think they must be reacting to his costume, and I'm embarrassed for Jonah. I recognize the pitch of their voices, quivering and wild, keening to respond to all that is masculine and quick to deride all that isn't masculine enough. The sound of feet rushes up behind us, then Jonah suddenly stops in his tracks, pulled back by a girl's foot set down hard on his unravelling bandages. More laughter, and I'm about the turn on them when I recognize one of the voices as Norah's.

I turn and step forward to kiss her on the cheek, but she shies away.

"Hi, Mom," she says.

The other girl lifts her foot from Jonah's bandages and he rebounds fully upright as though on an elastic band. He grins up at her foolishly. The girl laughs down at him. She is lithe, breathing lightly and fast, with waist-length shiny dark brown hair, and eyes that are just a little tilted, ending in sharp points. She's already made the transition to sleek dark clothes that make her appear as nervy and fast as a greyhound. She doesn't look at me until Norah says her name.

"Mariko and I were just going home to work on our Northwest Passage project."

The girl looks at me then, as if appraising whether or not I will give her trouble. "Together? I thought you were half done."

"New idea, Mom." Norah says. "Wait till you see the pictures."

"It'll be dark soon. This isn't really a good time to do homework. I need you to answer the door and hand out candy while I take Jonah around the block. Your Dad won't be home till late."

"I'm a crazy mummy," Jonah tells Mariko, waving his hands in circles around his head. The girl smiles out of the corner of her mouth, then runs the sharp point of her pink tongue along her upper lip. "I've got fangs," he tells her, lifting the candy teeth, holding them close to her face.

She says, "Ooooh. I'm scared."

"We're going out tonight," Norah tells me. "We're going to wear old clothes and be hobos." She says this with a hint of bravado.

Hobos, always the last costume of childhood, hastily thrown together at the last minute. So I know in my sinking heart that the innocent costumes have come to an end—the bunnies, fairies and butterflies I sewed by hand on the long afternoons when Jonah was a baby. I would have preferred her to open the door to little trick-or-treaters instead of wandering the night with blackened face, living by her wits from danger to danger.

"Then I need you to do door duty early. Come home with us now. Okay?"

The question at the end is new for me too, and I'm relieved when Norah and Mariko do that shuffling inarticulate dance of farewell that adolescents do when they accept the inevitable.

Once Mariko is out of earshot, Norah sounds more like the eager child she's always been. And she looks lighter on her feet, pixieish with her small pointed ears so receptive they poke out of her dark fine hair. She's talking excitedly.

"She told us there was a ghost downtown. There were burn marks on the walls and windows were cracked. Things were flying around."

"What are you talking about, Norah?"

"The ghost."

"Were you watching a movie?"

"No. It happened, it really happened, and the police have pictures. They came in the middle of the night and things were still flying around. It was in the newspaper."

"What newspaper?"

"*The National Enquirer*. Last year."

"Oh, well. That's not the most reputable source, Norah."

"But the police have pictures! And Mariko brought a Ouija board to school and we asked if the ghost was real and it said yes. And we asked it if . . . "

"Did your teacher know you were playing with a Ouija board?"

Norah grows suddenly quiet.

"She didn't know, did she?"

"No."

"Where were you?"

"In the washroom. At lunch time. We were allowed to stay in to help with the parties in the little kids' classes."

"Some help," I say. "Listen to me, Ouija boards are dangerous. They're part of a whole underworld of dark thoughts. You can get lost in that and never come back. And you'll scare younger kids half to death. Do you understand me?"

With some surprise, I realize these words are my mother's, delivered to me in the same tone of voice when I was exactly Norah's age. She's defensive now, carefully choosing her next words.

"She only let her friends play with it. We wouldn't let the little kids see."

This is the first I've heard of this particular friendship. Her name, Mariko, although unusual, sounds vaguely familiar. I remember something unsettling is associated with the name, but I've forgotten what it is.

"Do her parents let her take things like Ouija boards to school?"

"Her Dad died. And maybe it's not such a big deal to her mother. She has more important things to worry about," Norah says, very worldly. She's picked up the tone of my voice. She's not going to offer anything more. So I stop talking as we approach our driveway. I've grown wary too, and it's a shock that all this change arrived so suddenly on a walk home from the bus stop.

The front lawn has a new dead spot that seems to be growing night by night. My neighbours' lawns, too, have these round lunar patches of disturbed earth. It looks as though someone has been digging with a small shovel, flipping over grass, exposing the roots. Sometimes the crows are still here, hopping from place to place, turning over the sod even as we reach our property line but today they've retreated to the treetops where they caw and taunt each other. I turn saucer-sized clumps back into place and step on them with my shoe.

"These grubs are getting worse."

"Grubs?" Norah asks, scooting over and flipping the grass I've just pressed into place. "What do they look like?"

She's digging with her slender fingers into the cold dirt.

"They bury themselves deep in the ground. Fat white things curled like shrimp. They eat away the roots of the grass. And the crows come down and eat them in turn. Winter should kill them off."

"Wicked," Norah says, another change. A year ago she would have recoiled from anything slimy and ravenous.

Norah hangs around and helps me carve the pumpkin. I'm conscious of the sweet musky smell as we lift the lid, but she dives right in with her two hands. Norah scoops out the seeds like frog spawn, slippery and cool where they cling, wet, to the walls. But the flesh hums with an underground energy when we dig down into the pulp.

"Yuck. It's like the inside of a cold body," she says, obviously not too revolted. I see her slipping one seed into her mouth, chewing, then spitting out the hull.

I know just what she means. Norah was born by Caesarian section and I can't rake my fingernails through the slimy pulp of a jack-o-lantern without remembering what it was like to be scooped out like that, to be empty and sutured up in a tight line of pain. This year, she does most of the scraping. I get out an art book and we carve the jack-o-lantern to look like Edvard Munch's *The Scream*—a horrified stretched mouth and eyes that are long, panic-stricken holes letting out the light.

"Cool, Mom. This is our best pumpkin yet."

As I'm cleaning up I ask her, "Did you finish mapping the explorers' routes?"

"I'm not doing that anymore. What's the point? All those stupid men looking for something they'll never find. Has anyone ever made it through the Northwest Passage?"

"No, I don't think so. That was a dead end. And will be at least until global warming makes it a possibility. Maybe in your lifetime. Maps of the future could change more than they have since they said *dragons past this point.*"

"Did they really say that?"

"Yes, so you can see why most people would say they were incredibly brave—to head out like that without knowing where they were going."

"But that was the problem. They wanted the new world to be like the old one. Franklin's men went crazy dragging their silverware behind them in a lifeboat. Who needs silverware in the Arctic?"

"Maybe when you're in such an alien place, and it's so hopeless, you need the familiar more than the practical," I say, amazed that we're even having a conversation this sophisticated. She's still too young to feel pity, yet she's old enough to ridicule the misfortune of adults, thinking that they are somehow marked for it.

"Mariko told me that the Franklin expedition was poisoned by lead in the tin cans for their food. The officers had the best food, so they went crazy first. The last ones alive had to eat each other. There were knife marks on their leg bones, from silverware." And she laughs in a new way, a suppressed snuffle of cynicism.

She fishes a book out of her bag. I see the title quickly, *Frozen in Time*, but I jump when she flashes the first photo of a corpse before my eyes.

"My God, Norah, you could have warned me." It's a photo of a young man tied down in a narrow coffin, a kerchief wrapped tight under his chin, yet the lips are curled back in a snarl, the eyes are half open, the irises icy disks of milky blue with no pupils. His big toes are tied together, the hands tied by strips of cloth knotted around his body at knees and hips. Even though he looks as though he could spring dangerously to life, his hands are heartbreaking in their slenderness.

"This is John Torrington." She flips through the book. "And this is John Hartnell," but I've turned away after one glimpse of that eyeless socket.

"Where did you get that?"

"From Mariko."

"Well, give it back! I don't want Jonah seeing it."

"Mom, these were the lucky ones, with graves and plaques, and the people around them digging down into the permafrost so they wouldn't be forgotten. Don't you wonder about the rest? The ones without the graves?"

"No, I don't. Dead and buried," I say, trying to sound certain.

"Not buried. Don't you want to know what happened to them? What they had to do to stay alive?"

"No. I'm taking Jonah now. Put that book away and answer the door."

I replenish Jonah's costume in the bathroom, wrapping him in more toilet paper. He asks this time for the ends to hang down.

"My ghost is trailing behind me, like a shadow," he tells me swishing from side to side, and the lengths of toilet paper drift on currents of air from his movement.

"Don't say that."

He stops swishing and looks at me with incomprehension.

"I'm just superstitious," I say, kissing him. He's delighted by the lipstick we dab to redden the whiteness. He wants lipstick on his lips, and I put some on myself as well and kiss him again, loudly on one cheek, leaving my mark there as we head out into the night.

"There, now you're Mommy's mummy," I say and he laughs. We complete the block in record time because his legs are that much longer than last year. And like last year, he can't be coaxed up the driveway to the house where recorded whale song is blaring out of speakers near the front door. The wailing, clicking, hysterical underwater laughter makes him cling to my side, saying, "I don't want to hear the wild voices. Mommy, it's too wild." After that, he loses his enthusiasm and stops every ten feet to rifle around in his bag of candy, which is growing heavy, though he won't let me carry it for him.

We keep to the edges, but coming down the street, right in the middle, is a tall girl, unconcerned with traffic that might come up behind her. She is wearing a long white dress and has silver tinsel tied throughout her long hair and attached to her shoulders and along her arms. The wind picks up her silver hair and blows it around her face as we pass.

So this is what happens, I think, recognizing her foolhardy willingness to take on the world, even as it rushes up dangerously from behind. Norah's harsh judgment of the Franklin expedition tells me that she already thinks she can do better.

"I swear it's colder since that girl passed by," I tell Jonah. "Let's go home."

IAN IS HOME and Norah is not. Ian tells me she left with her new friend, Mariko, their faces blackened with burnt cork, but little else in the way of costumes. He laughs. I can smell the singed smell of old wine cork still hanging in the kitchen.

"Did you think it was wise to let her go out with Mariko?"

He looks puzzled when I tell him that I don't think Mariko is a very good influence and maybe we should discourage the friendship while we still can. I've remembered where I heard her name before.

"She's the girl whose father was found frozen last winter. Remember? The man who committed suicide by the river? Her mother lost it after that, so the girl just comes and goes."

"Poor kid. Sounds like she could use a harbour in the storm," he says. But I remember something else.

"She was in a fight last summer in the park. She was the girl who hit the older boy in the nose and drew blood. Remember that gang of kids egging things on? That was her, in the middle of it."

He laughs. "So why did she punch the kid in the nose?"

"I don't know, and I don't want to know," I say.

Instead of making him averse, however, I see when Mariko and Norah return with their pillowcases full of loot that Ian is intrigued.

He watches Mariko slip out of the dark suit jacket he lent her for her hobo costume, a voluptuous little shrug.

After Mariko leaves, I hear him downstairs asking Norah about the fight last summer, whether that was her friend. I ease down the top three stairs to hear their conversation.

"Yes, but they were making fun of her," Norah answers, a little evasive.

"Why would they do that? She seems like a sweet girl. And she's so pretty."

"I love her long hair," Norah says, sounding smitten. "I wish my hair was long like hers. She never gets it cut because her mother's sick, you know. She has to rest all the time and can't take her anywhere." After a pause, she says, "They were teasing Mariko about it."

"About her long hair?"

"No, about her mother being sick."

"Why would they care?"

Norah sighs in a slightly exasperated way and says, "Because they could see the Christmas tree through the window with its needles all brown and they thought it was weird."

"That is a little weird, for July," he says.

"I know. Mariko threw it out after that. I helped her. We dragged it into the woods when no one was looking. And we found a fort some boys built."

THE NEXT AFTERNOON, Mariko and Norah are already there at the kitchen table when I arrive home with Jonah. They have made colour copies on the scanner of the photos of the open graves from the Franklin expedition and have them spread around on the table where we're going to eat, in clear view. Norah quickly flips over the ones she showed me yesterday of the men in their coffins before Jonah has his boots off, but photos of the gravesite itself are left face up. I catch sight of the most desolate, lifeless landscape I could ever imagine: small grey stones, drift ice and water so weirdly chemically blue, it looks as though it could burn the flesh right off your bones. The graves are all oriented the same direction, not towards inland mountains or sea, but looking down the endless ugly beach, disturbed only by the gravel mounds of larger stones holding the dead down, intact.

"What did I tell you yesterday, Norah," I say. I say nothing to Mariko.

"Mom, we *are* being careful. Jonah wasn't even here!"

That night, I don't sleep easily. I see a man dressed in a good overcoat and tie flattening the snow before taking off his shoes and lying down. I see the slow removal of clothing, skin against snow. I see the fixed discoloured faces of those open graves of the Franklin expedition. I can't get the images out of my mind and I'm exhausted by morning.

MARIKO STILL DOESN'T SPEAK to me directly, never meets my eye, but she does seem more girlish. I can see what Norah sees in her. There's a mischievous quality to her, a springy energy in her body, a readiness to laugh that is surprising, given the circumstances of her life. I take the girls to the video store on the weekend. Mariko keeps Norah between herself and me, doesn't look me in the eye. I'm surprised to notice that she's my height, breathing a higher, more energized layer of oxygen than my still childlike daughter. Their project must be completed and handed in, although I don't ask. The Franklin expedition is suddenly off-limits as a topic of conversation. We finally agree *2001: A Space Odyssey*, which I haven't seen since I was their age. Norah is dubious about the choice, thinks it's hopelessly old-fashioned, but goes along with me to keep peace. Mariko reads the back of the video and says, "Wicked." So that's where Norah got that word. Norah decides to be happy about the choice.

I wait for them to go downstairs to the den with popcorn, Mariko dashing ahead of Norah. Then I head out the door, straight through the backyard, past the boundary line of our housing development to the place Jonah described to me at breakfast. A place in the forest they've taken him to without my permission. His directions are surprisingly accurate. I ease myself down and up a dirt trench that will be a new sewer system and cross a ravine, then enter the trees. Their branches are bare, tangled and dark above me. Here and there tree limbs are punctuated with clumps of leaves and branches—crows' nests. Now you can see what they've been up to when they were hidden away all summer. Light reaches the ground like something unhealthy, charged with bright radiation. The leaves underfoot are not quite as crisp and pungent as they were even a week ago. They are starting to freeze and crumble unpleasantly under my feet.

I move down into a basin of trees, mostly oak and poplar, and see the bright green slash on the opposite slope. As I draw closer, the unnatural green turns out to be a piece of astroturf covering plywood that forms the roof of a bunker-like fort. It is quite sophisticated, with a long rectangular opening for spying or gun barrels, obviously built with care and planning. Jonah told me they were given the fort by some boys, and remembering last summer's fight in the park, I wonder what Mariko had to do to seize control of this prime piece of real estate. I'm already thinking of it as hers. I have to squat to enter, steel myself against the musty odour of damp earth, waiting for my eyes to adjust to the darkness. Then things come into focus.

The fort is neat and organized. Set upon a low plank table propped up with concrete blocks is china in a floral pattern, far too good to be offered up for play, candles in pottery holders. Beside the table is a Tupperware box weighed down with *Seventeen* magazines. Inside is a cache of food: chips, tins of luncheon meat, crackers and canned soft drinks. I also find some of my old lipsticks and compacts, and a travelling mirror. There's a little whisk and dustpan leaning against the earth wall. All is innocent, except for the candles, which I've tried to discourage Norah from lighting in her room. A fire would turn this small underground space into a crematorium.

I lift a man's dark overcoat from the floor in the corner and catch my breath when I see a Ouija board underneath. Set down in the centre of the board are house keys on a gold key chain, a man's red silk neck tie and a photograph. It's a graduation shot, the man is smiling widely, triumphant. The matte is embossed with the words University of Waterloo, Doctorate of Mathematics, probably a foreign student here on scholarship, a family's pride and joy. He doesn't look much older than Mariko. I've caught a sense of him on his coat, intimate and lightly scented with aftershave. These objects may be all of him she has now. I don't know what to do. For a moment, I'm frozen, but I leave them where I found them.

When I get home, I can hear their laughter travelling through the registers of the house. Gales of laughter, winding up into near hysteria so that Norah's voice, or is it Mariko's, is a high cry. Far below the high pitch of their voices is another voice, deep in tone, a blurred drunken sound. Terrifying, that slow motion man's voice saying something over and over I can't distinguish. I take my shoes off and slip down the stairs, listen at the closed door of the den. There is definitely a man's voice, buried at short intervals by the uncontrollable laughter of the two girls.

"I can feel it," he's saying. "I can feel it." He repeats the same line in an insinuating voice slowing down. I open the door quickly.

The room smells strange, something chemical with a sickening hint of banana burning the hairs inside my nose. They are rewinding the video, playing it, and rewinding it again.

"What is that strong smell?" I ask, surprising them. Norah suddenly pauses the video, cutting the sound. They are each holding an open bottle of nail polish in their hands: one purple, one blue. Their feet are bare and the toenails on each foot have been painted alternating colours. These macabre shades are a far cry from the strawberry pink Norah puts on her fingernails for special occasions.

"Where did you get this nail polish?"

"It's Mariko's. What's wrong?" Norah looks alarmed.

"Your pupils look dilated." I open the window high up on the wall and an icy blast slaps me in the face. I inhale and wait, my hands on the sill near my shoulders, trying to decide what to do. But I wait a moment too long. When I turn around, they are gone, and then I hear them talking to Ian upstairs, at first quietly, but then Norah's voice returns to normal and I hear her laugh like a girl. Ian is cajoling her about something and I leave them to it, go through the door to the garage.

My hands are cold. I forgot my gloves inside and don't want to go back in, not yet, while my heart is still beating too fast. I stand on the edge of the lunar circle on the front lawn, which is suddenly more difficult to see. Just in the last few days, the grass has changed from green to a smoky grey.

When I come inside, Jonah is sitting on Mariko's lap, and she's reading him a story. It's his favourite, *Sitting Ducks*, about alligators that run a duck factory. I move around in the kitchen, trying to keep busy as I listen. She pauses between words, nuzzling into his neck as she reads. "The alligator acted...friendly, but all the while he was thinking...what a delicious meal the duck would make when properly...fattened," she's saying. Jonah knows where the switch takes place, when the alligator becomes a friend of the little duck. She says, "Look at this picture, Jonah. It's so cute." They have turned to the page with the duck and the alligator curled up in bed together.

Mariko asks, "Do you ever get scared in your bed at night?" I can hear the loneliness in her voice, and it makes me feel suddenly ashamed. Jonah must hear it too. He turns and puts his arms around her neck.

"Wait till you find out what happens, Mariko. The ducks all fly south," he tells her.

"Oh, that's good. I'd fly south if I could. Especially to get away from hungry alligators." And she tickles him.

IAN TURNS AWAY from me in his sleep. I touch his bare shoulder, but he doesn't move. Either he is lying awake in the dark, as I am, or he is beyond me and cannot feel my hand. The faint, far-off sound of the girls' voices rises through the ductwork, preventing me from falling asleep, and once the wave of sleepiness has passed, something else keeps me lying here, staring up at the blades of the ceiling fan, still and slightly warped, like the propellers of a boat. Pushing darkness down over my face.

The house is quiet now, but I get up to pace the hallway, back and forth, without turning on the light. Then I ease down to the kitchen. I don't plan to move on towards the basement stairs, then I do, stepping quietly from one stair to the next so that the girls don't hear me. The door of the den is open and I look inside.

They are side by side, asleep on the pullout bed. I ease closer till I'm standing over them. I can make out the curtain of Mariko's hair falling across her face, Norah's slender hand hanging over the edge of the bed, the length of her bare arm. She seems to be tucked down and curled against Mariko. I can smell an unfamiliar smell, the smell of a stranger, and the sweet essence of Norah too. Once my eyes adjust to the different kind of darkness in the basement, I see that the two of them have at least some space between them. Norah is wearing a T-shirt instead of pajamas, something she's never done before. Mariko, too, is wearing one of Norah's oversize T-shirts, I think the violet one, but it's hard to tell. Everything has neutralized to shades of grey and black.

Mariko starts to breathe more quickly, almost an anxious pant. I back away quickly, fearing that she senses my presence in the room. She settles again and I take just one minute more to look at Norah, who is sleeping with the otherworldly peace of a girl in a fairy tale. I'll be watching from a distance now as her prettiness matures into something more potent.

Ian must have known that I didn't sleep much because he leaves me in bed in the morning. I do sleep a little, drifting in and out as the house comes to life and the smells of breakfast cooking, a full company kind of breakfast, smoky bacon, eggs, toast, ease in under the door. The voices downstairs are animated. Ian is obviously going to some effort to welcome this girl. I pretend I'm asleep when he opens the door. I feel him approach the bed, then withdraw. Then, I hear the laughter and high spirits lift again downstairs. He's laughing along with the girls at something uproarious.

Norah sees me and calls out, "Mom. Wait till you see Jonah. He—," but I interrupt her.

"Norah, your voice is going right through my head. I have a splitting headache."

"Wait a minute. There's getting up on the wrong side of the bed and then there's getting up on—," Ian says. I hear the jocularity in his voice, the confident, cajoling tone.

"Shut up, Ian. Just shut up."

Then there is silence. Mariko, still wearing Norah's T-shirt over her black jeans, keeps her eyes down. Norah has her arms across her chest, and is biting her lip, face turned to the wall. Jonah shuffles over to me. I haven't noticed until now that he's wrapped himself in layers of toilet paper, wrapped it thickly around his legs, arms and torso in a crude replica of his Halloween costume. He must have used every roll he could find in the bathroom. It is particularly thick around his middle, but it has slipped down and hangs from him in the back like a dirty diaper. The ends of the roll are dangling from his arms and dragging behind him. Lengths of toilet paper break off with every step. He's shredding before my eyes.

"Mom, I want my ghost cup." When Jonah is sick or afraid, he wants the cup that he had when he was a toddler, with the two handles and weight in the base. He calls it his ghost cup because he thinks it's spooky the way it always bounces back into an upright position no matter how you hold it down. This is a sure sign that I've upset him, but I can't soothe him now.

"Jonah, you're too old for that cup and you're too old to be making such a mess. Whose idea was it for you to waste all this toilet paper?" He starts to cry.

"I just want to be alone right now," I say. Jonah looks at me, frightened. Then I can hear him snuffling in the hall. Mariko and Norah leave next, taking the stairs to the basement. Ian starts towards the hallway where Jonah is but he stops for one moment, face close to mine. He's menacing and quiet.

"You're really losing it. I'm going to talk to our son now, then I'm going to talk to our daughter. Then it will be your turn."

I'm tired, my head feels thick, and there's an undercurrent of nausea that threatens to grow stronger. I turn the front burner of the stove on high, fill the kettle at the sink, hold back the curtain to look out the window at the front lawn. Good, I think, the two circles of damage done by the grubs haven't grown any larger. Even overnight, the chemicals seem to be working. Perhaps Tylenol can do the same for my head, tightening now with strengthening concentric circles of pain.

I'm upstairs with the headache pills in my hand when I hear screams. So piercing, I can't tell who they're coming from. By the time I reach the kitchen, Mariko has Jonah down on the floor, the tablecloth has been pulled off the table, scattering dirty dishes all over, and the room is filling up with acrid smoke. He's screaming beneath her and I rush to pull her off. Norah is screaming too.

"Mom, Mom, do something. He's on fire."

Mariko has him wrapped in the tablecloth rolled tight beneath her, holding him down, her arms around him. I can't see any flames. He's still sobbing, but starts to quiet down as she says over and over, "It's okay. It's okay. You're okay."

Floating in the air and settling on the kitchen floor are wispy black ashes, some in the shape of squares floating down to the floor and then I understand what has happened. Norah is closer than I am. I tell her, "Turn off the stove, Norah. Don't touch that melted cup." The filled kettle still sits harmlessly on the counter where I left it.

Jonah's pink face emerges from beneath Mariko's shoulder. Some of his hair has been singed, but he doesn't seem to be in pain.

"I think he's all right now, Mariko. The fire's out," I say, calmer than I've felt in days.

Ian has rushed into the kitchen and gently moves Mariko aside. He unwraps Jonah from the tablecloth, slowly, carefully. Most of the toilet paper has burned away. He peels away the pieces that remain. Here and there whole lengths of toilet paper are untouched, but most of it falls away, charred ashes in his hands. Jonah's pajamas, covered with shooting rockets, seem to be intact although sooty.

The fire retardant permeating the fabric has done its job. Ian holds Jonah on his lap on the floor, checks his hands and feet, moves Jonah's sleeves up, finding nothing but pale flawless skin.

"Does it hurt anywhere?" he asks.

"Here," Jonah says, holding his palms to his eyebrows.

We all breathe again. I move to open the window and a limitless world of cool oxygen starts to make its way into the smoky kitchen.

"A miracle," Ian says. "You are one lucky kid."

"That paper burned so fast, it saved him," I say, but then consider how ungrateful this sounds. "With Mariko's help."

The shirt Mariko borrowed from Norah the night before has melt holes in it and she's pulling it away from her chest in vague attempts at modesty.

"Get Mariko the comforter from your bed, Norah. Are you burned anywhere?" I ask her. She looks at me uncertainly, shakes her head no, but reaches up and touches her burnt hair. She half smiles at me wistfully.

"How did you know what to do?" I ask her.

"I didn't. Everything happened so fast," she says and I realize that this is the first thing she has ever said to me directly. Her hair is burned on the left side, singed inches shorter than it was, melted like dolls' hair near her shoulder. She adds, "I was waiting for Norah to come upstairs and Jonah dragged the chair over. He climbed up to get something out of the cupboard and then his costume went on fire. Just like that."

"I was frozen. I was so scared, Mom, I was frozen," Norah says.

THE SNOW STARTED to fall in the morning. By lunchtime, the world has transformed into a swirling white void, the sky a deeper grey than all that lies below, as though the world is reversed, a photo negative. The ground, the lawn, the trees, the usually dark street are a vivid intense white. All the ugliness of the morning and the days before have receded and the house is full of a holiday atmosphere, a joyful excitement. An unexpected storm rages outside of this safe house. Fire has not claimed any one of us. The girls are high-spirited, dancing with abandon in the living room, their music, *Our Lady Peace*, turned up loud. Mariko's newly shortened hair, from the haircut I gave her this morning, whips around her face. Ian sees that the house cannot contain them much longer and sends them out for milk we do not need, giving them an excuse to confront the elements directly.

"Your mission, if you choose to accept it," he tells them, "is to traverse this unknown land. There will be dangers—barrens where only the strongest survive. Polar bears will lurk behind every mailbox, fierce storms continue to rage. You will be tested by the harshest conditions known to man. Oh sorry," he says, "known to girl. You will have to find your way without maps or the protection of the motherland. You will be alone, your very mettle tested. Are you up to it?" he asks them as they giggle, and Norah jumps up and down saying. "Yes! Yes!"

I expect that they will walk to the store, meandering from yard to yard, tasting snow in their open mouths. But, too late to stop them, I see them skidding down the driveway on their bicycles, howling like wolves, circling around in the street, whooping, hollering, careening crazily in front of the house until they set off, leaving serpentine trails behind them. This is the way it will be from now on. I will sit by the window and if they turn around, they will not be able to see me. I will pray for safe passage as they reach the corner, their shapes dissolved by blowing snow, and disappear into the storm.

Endowment

A HAND SOFTLY ALIGHTS ON MY SHOULDER when I'm standing in a shopping mall listening to a children's choir switch tracks from the *Huron Carol* to the schmaltzy *It's a Marshmallow World*. Good thing, too, because I always feel tears rising when I hear a children's choir at Christmas. Their red satin robes sway in unison. I turn to see who has touched me. So familiar is the exact weight of the touch that I think it must be my first love, whom I haven't laid eyes on since he left me exhausted at a Metro stop in Montreal twenty years ago. But it's not. It's his mother.

I smile and his mother smiles back at me. We've both been swept up by time and set down miraculously here in this ugly cavernous slush-stained corridor looking shockingly changed. Instead of her lush, thick, pageboy haircut, she's wearing a white turban-like hat and pale wraparound coat so that she seems to be here, in a public place, mistakenly in her bathrobe. Her face is thinner and more haunted and her eyes seem larger and darker than I remember them. Maybe it's the ghastly light that's taken the colour out of her face. But her voice is exactly the same.

"Marylee! Merry, Marylee, quite contrary, how are you? Who are you now?"

I hug her hard, my heart pounding with the surprise of it, thrilled by her directness, which was part of her subversive charm when I was little more than a child.

"That doesn't rhyme properly, you know."

"Oh, who cares? How are you?"

And I find myself listing my accomplishments as though I've been waiting 20 years for the opportunity to graduate from the basement of her home where the only accomplishment I cared anything about was having an orgasm without getting pregnant—not always a given when your partner is also seventeen. A simple pill would have remedied this but I never did seek out that liberating prescription for reasons he just couldn't understand. And neither could I, not really.

This is how the list goes and I tick off things in my mind as I talk: University. India, doing good. Law school. All the immigration stuff. Pro bono.

"Darling, you've been wonderfully productive. I always knew you had that in you. Any children?"

I shake my head and pause. The choir has been singing *O Little Town of Bethlehem* and I tear up. Then one lone boy's voice rises above the rest on the words "the hopes and fears of all our years" and I feel a catch in my throat, then, horrified, I emit a little sob.

"Sorry. It's the Christmas carols and children's voices."

She's hugging me again, stroking my hair, then cupping the back of my skull as though I'm an infant with a wobbly neck.

"Yes, we all need to watch out for the children. I'm sorry I asked you that. Please forgive me," she murmurs into my ear.

We pull apart and I look into her eyes, realizing why they look so different. Just wispy pale eyebrows and dusky-coloured eyelids. Half-moons of delicate violet rest under her eyes. But there's nothing sparkly in the colour, not makeup, but a buildup of pigment in the cells around her brown eyes.

I can see that she's sizing me up for my femaleness, an appraising glance I remember well from her son. *Will she give me what I want?* is what that gaze means. This last thought has only occurred to me now, decades after my relationship with her son is over. I'm in the process of extricating myself from yet another relationship game of "come here: go away" and thinking about where the pattern started. With her son, of course,

"Well, you've been busy. No wonder. It's not too late."

We both turn back to listen to the choir, now singing *In the Bleak Midwinter* in complicated harmony, children concentrating hard, watching their conductor with unblinking eyes. Then the audience around us breaks into applause and I jump a little. I have been so focused on her, that's all I could ever call her, even though she asked me to use her first name, Janine, years ago. *Her, she,* the mother so unlike my mother. Why would she need a name? The world shrinks to the two of us and that choir of children's voices. I forget we are discussing such intimacies in the midst of Christmas shoppers.

The dispersal of the crowd seems to make both of us more inhibited. We establish a few essential facts about our lives, quickly, in telegraph form. That I'm back in Ottawa, a special human rights position at the university. No need to mention the man in Toronto who didn't ask me to reconsider my move.

She's still living in the family home but Joseph is in long-term care. Dementia, I must have realized how much older than her he was back then, too hard for her to handle, first he was volatile, angry at her, and she couldn't take it, now he loses himself in the slow lapping enjoyment of a vanilla ice cream cone, if she can get it to his room before it melts. She hates to see his tongue coated with it but it's worth the peaceful visit. But not chocolate. He throws chocolate against the wall. She laughs.

After a minute of us looking at each other and smiling, almost conspiratorial, she adds, "Oh, and ovarian cancer. I almost forgot, thank God. Just for one minute I like to forget."

Too shocked to address this bleak fact yet, I continue with the questions.

"And Shae, how is he? Is he here for Christmas?"

"No, dear, he never is. He's in Nigeria. You know what a traveler he is. We wanted him to feel free, but I guess the leash was a little too long. He's lived abroad for over 15 years and really can't stand the Canadian climate any more. He never comes home just to visit, but sometimes for work. Should have put flypaper on the threshold, if I wanted my family to stick."

So this is how I end up promising to come visit her on Christmas Eve, in the late afternoon, before the onslaught of nieces and nephews and talk of breastfeeding and too much food that increasingly characterizes my own family at Christmas. Last year, they even bundled up the kids and created an ad hoc caroling group to blitz their friends in the neighbourhood, something I definitely want to miss.

IT'S ALREADY DARK when she opens the door to welcome me in and I'm hit with a wave of nostalgia, the smell in her house is so familiar. A little musty, but alive. It smells like Shae did all those years ago. I feel an echo of longing to slip down the basement stairs to the old couch next to the good sound system, the loom like some fantastic torture device standing off in the dark recesses of the unfinished basement, with its strings all open and waiting for the shuttle tossed back and forth to create the weft of the fabric, the nubbly, animal-smelling bumps and lumps of the final texture. Something purple and red half-made, stretched out tight. What do I remember of those nights of my adolescence? That he smelled like a river, wet stone, cold currents. He smelled like freshness and life, and his feet were warm against my legs, his mouth so sweet against my chilled skin as my top came off.

We sit together on the couch, with my mother's lemon squares on a bone-china plate untouched. She's unwrapping a present I had originally wrapped for my mother—a large silk scarf of reds and yellows in a traditional Indian design that I picked up at the Bangalore airport. It was meant to be worn as a head cover with a *salwar khameez* and although my mother would have exclaimed with pleasure that she loved my exotic gifts, she wouldn't have been up to the complicated length, the loose loops several times around her neck she would need in order to wear it well. She would have left it abandoned in the back of a drawer.

Janine, the name I'm forcing myself to call her, pulls the pale turban-like scarf from her head after shaking the silk free of the wrapping paper.

"Oh, how beautiful," she says. "I love red."

I'm trying to keep my face blandly pleasant, as though her bald head is the most natural thing in the world, the bumps, grey bristles here and there, the way her elfin ears seem to stick out, the cartilage along the tops so thin it is almost completely unrolled.

"I remember that piece of weaving you were working on in the basement all those years ago. Mostly red. Did you ever finish it?" I ask.

"It took years, but I did. Shae has it now, but his wife, Karen, won't hang it. She says it would be a hatchery for moths and beetles in Lagos." She's frowning a little, but starts to wrap the silk expertly around her head, the layers of it gently softening her skull. She tucks in the end and it's perfect.

"I've had plenty of practice," she answers before I've even asked the question. "Going on two years of chemo now. I forget what it feels like to brush my hair. But it won't be too much longer."

"So, you're almost done treatment. Two years is an awfully long time."

"I'll never be done."

I'm confused, but leave it.

She reaches across and hugs me hard again, forcing my chin into her bony shoulder, almost cutting off my breath.

"It's so good to see you again. You're just as beautiful as you were at 17."

We're sitting side by side and I look at my hands in my lap, reluctant to meet her eye. Then she's stroking my hair. Her hand pulls my hair into a gentle ponytail, slides along to the ends near my collar before settling again, gently, near my crown.

SOON SHE'S SHOWING me a photo album and I squint to see how my first love, Shae, has aged since I last saw him. The red hair seems brown now, not so luxurious and certainly not so long. Now he looks as world-weary as the rest of us. Ordinary, with dull receding hair and thin forearms.

"After he had the baby, he changed. He started to wonder about the other children he might have fathered. You know how he was."

"What do you mean?"

"You know he had a wild side. When he first got to Nigeria, he was single. And the women he met had no inhibitions."

That sounds a little racist, which surprises me. She was such a down-with-American-imperialism type, so my mother told me, when it started to be more about the banks than bombs. She seems to be reading my mind, anticipates my reaction before I've decided if I actually want to express it.

"Yes, some African women, but I really meant other aid workers. International development work is like the war was for the older generation, but you must know this from your own travels. Life is short and they're all in it together so why not give it a whirl?"

She turns the page and I see a photo of a blonde woman with Shae, delicately smiling, definitely shy. She's leaning into Shae's underarm and he grasps her protectively. He's smiling frankly, with none of the evasiveness of adolescence. He looks happy.

"That's Karen. She wasn't exactly an aid worker. She was a secretary here in Ottawa. They married fast, before he went back and he took her with him."

This last part leads her to flip quickly through some pages of the album she doesn't care to show me. Does she think I'll be hurt by his wedding photos? I'm surprised something like that could even occur to her after so many years.

"Oh, I'm being politically incorrect. They're not secretaries any more. They are administrators. Or assistants. Something like that."

She closes that album, and pulls another from the shelf.

"Here, let's look at this one. I have a few photos of you and Shae. Remember that weekend we skied into the cottage?"

WE PARKED AT THE WIDEST part of a dirt road, just before a little bridge that spanned a mostly frozen stream. The forest across the field was smoky blue, a solid wall of spruce and snow. His Dad was going to pull a sleigh of food and supplies—the dried beans, odd lumpy vegetables with names I didn't yet know, bottles of red wine and heavy brown breads that were unfamiliar. My mother still liked white bread with the crusts cut off. There was no trail into the cottage. In summer, they came by canoe, the smaller-sized yellow one I saw hanging in their garage and a large one, almost a war canoe, that I had only seen in photos, with his mother standing at the prow with her arms raised like a conductor. In the photo, she looked as though she was singing.

His parents conferred in the front seat with a contour map and compass, working out a route to the cottage. His mother, Janine, whose name I couldn't bring myself to use as I was directed to, was high-spirited and argumentative about the best route.

"We have to climb here," she jabbed at the map, "or else we'll end up stranded in the swamp."

I was delighted by all this drama because it made our outing seem more like an expedition with inherent dangers, a true adventure with risks although I had the feeling that they always followed the same route every winter, that the map and compass and passionate debate were part of heightening the experience, undertaken for the sake of an audience. I'm pretty sure I was the first girlfriend, but it could have been anyone they bestowed this gift on.

They folded up the map, resolved on the route, made a production of waxing the skis, with purple under the foot and blue to the tips. His father leaned into the corking of the skis as I stood near the car, trying not to let them see me shiver, wanting them to believe that I could be as worldly as they were, up to anything the day threw at us—swamps, dead ends, the need to be rescued in a blizzard by helicopter. Finally, I was snapped into an old pair of his mother's skis, and we set off, wobbly at first but it didn't take long before I got the hang of it. And before I knew it, we left the forest and crossed the frozen lake, the cold wind in our faces. The cottage stood alone on the far shore and there wasn't another sign that any other human had ever even found this lake on a map. Then the cottage, more of a house really, stood tall above us. His mother had told me in the car that the cottage had been lovingly reconstructed from logs from an old farmhouse in another county.

"We had the logs brought over by boat, one by one, from the boat launch on the next lake. There's a secret way in, just for us," Janine said. "Of course, we had to make the windows larger. The first old log houses used heavy oiled paper for glass. Did you know that, Marylee?"

"No, I didn't."

"Well, no one could read then and it was off to bed with the sun so it didn't matter," Janine told her. "Look at those beautiful windows!" Janine said. "They're from the last TB sanitorium in the Ottawa Valley. Storm windows too. They used to leave patients out on these glassed-in porches, even in winter. Imagine!"

I knew it made me sound like a naïve child, so I was careful to keep anything querulous out of my tone, "Where are the closest neighbours?"

"Not on this lake! No motorboat-loving, hotdog-chomping, beer-slugging, radio-blasting cretins within five miles. We bought the whole lake. The last of the original homesteaders was in a nursing home. Private sale. We got it for a song."

"Come on Shae, join in on the hiking song," his father said, suddenly hearty.

"Dad, if you want to sing it, go ahead. We're here and I'm not five years old," Shae said.

She did hear his Dad singing outside while he was chopping wood for the wood stove, an old song she heard long ago, not knowing the words. She almost laughed at the corny accent, so unfamiliar. His father didn't have a lot to say, but he was usually very precise and scientific, just as she would have expected from an engineer who studied aircraft design in the wind tunnel at the National Research Council.

When I was young I used to wait
On the boss and hand him his plate
And pass down the bottle when he got dry
And brush away the blue tail fly

Jimmy crack corn and I don't care
Jimmy crack corn and I don't care
Jimmy crack corn and I don't care
My master's gone away.

Shae's mother lit the oil lanterns, then the wood stove, and until it finally got warm, the snow we tracked in and swept from our shoulders glittered on the dark wood floor like silver filigree in the honey-coloured light. Our breath froze and fell as tiny crystals onto the round oak table.

Shae nudged the small of my back with his elbow and I followed his eyes to the massive wood stove that was starting to tick as the metal warmed up. *Master Climax* was written on it in happy script, a long-ago innocent brand name.

"Your wish is my command," he whispered to me, but instead of giggling, I stepped away from him.

His mother noticed and came over to me, smoothed my hair with her hands and kissed my forehead. She had never done this before. The impression left by her warm lips tingled cold for a long time. I had the feeling that she left a lipstick mark on me but couldn't check. There were no mirrors anywhere.

Once the downstairs was starting to get warm, she led us up the stairs and left us alone in the room with the one double bed, across the hall from their own. She had pointed out the wrought-iron vent in the floor.

"This is the warmest room," she said. "And the most private."

"What's wrong?" Shae asked me once she'd gone back downstairs.

I was standing just inside the room, calming myself by tracing with my eyes the Mexican zigzag motif of the bedspread, woven in reds and yellows intersected by thin lines of lightning blue. It must have been made by his mother on her big loom in the basement.

I wondered why the loom's hulking shape, the shadowy corners of the unfinished cellar were such an aphrodisiac but this lovely bedroom, tacit approval of his parents, and accoutrements of a rustic B&B were so intimidating.

He saw me looking at the bed and said, "Yeah, it's little weird. For me too."

"They're right there across from us. I couldn't."

He came up behind me and nestled his face in my hair. "They won't come in. They never come downstairs at home. You know that."

He wrapped his arms around me from behind, his palm cupping my left breast. But I could hear his mother downstairs, cast iron frying pan against cast iron stove. It sounded like a giant bell. I felt myself stiffening.

"You have to admit, it's a bit of a waste. I hoped we could sneak away and here we are, given a room for the night."

"I just can't. Not here. Not now."

"Okay, okay, but I've never really gotten it. You do everything else, we both get off all the time, but not that. What's so great about being a virgin?"

"I don't think of myself as a virgin. That's just a technicality."

"Technicality. You sound like a lawyer."

I felt a familiar resistance to him that I couldn't explain. Something about not being subsumed. Something about not being too available and losing track of my own desires and aspirations. I never assumed we would stay together, and we didn't, but it wasn't until summer that we broke up. In another city where he was working in a restaurant kitchen, we had a fight that started in a stranger's apartment on Peel Street and went on, his will pitted against mine, the whole evening until he delivered me to the metro stop so I could catch a Greyhound back to Ottawa. He sent me down the wrong stairway first and stood across the tracks from me on the opposite platform, gesticulating, pointing at his feet. I was so offended, I pretended I didn't know him, and soon enough, I didn't.

"No means no," I said, suddenly stubborn, the seeds of our summer fight being sowed in a gorgeous rustic bedroom on the wintry lake. Even a year later, that would have been the most irresistibly erotic situation. The oil lamp his mother lit created a number of golden halos: oblong on ivory lace curtains, circular with a dark heart on the rough squared beams of the ceiling above us.

"Now you really do sound like a lawyer," he said.

"And what do you sound like? A wheedling jerk. Soon you'll be telling me it really really hurts."

His mother called up the stairs, something about wine and dinner being ready in a little while. It could have gone either way, and he chose the easier path.

"Okay. We'll just hang a blanket between us like a courting couple back on the homestead. We'll bundle, if that's what you want."

We spent the night under the blankets, fully clothed. I don't even think we kissed. He was mostly turned on his side, away from me. The night was windless and quiet, not a bird or tick of snow against the window, no electric hum. I wondered if his parents were lying awake in their room or if they'd already fallen asleep. A while later, I heard his mother's voice low and broken, as though she was crying. What hidden sorrow was she expressing, but then both their voices got louder, rhythmic, in unison.

SHE'S SHOWING ME another album, not noticing how distracted I've been. Shae as a baby wearing a white matching sweater set, Shae in a basin, splashing water on the kitchen table.

"When he was born, the doctor said, 'He's going to make some woman very happy.' I'm so glad you're here to talk to. Most other people wouldn't understand, but you could handle it. You were such a little slip of a girl at seventeen, I wondered if his endowment would scare you off."

I may be 37 years old, but she's shocked me. I feel as though I'm back at the cottage, warding off sexual pressure.

"Maybe I didn't handle it."

She laughs. "So now you tell me! All my hopes for you were for naught." She wags her index finger at me as though I really have been a bad little girl.

The truth was I was relieved when my long-term lovers after him were a better fit. In every way, the men who followed suited me better. Although there was never another mother like his. I realized, rapt as I was by her cheekbones and upturned lips, that I'd been pining for her ever since my teens.

"I waited a long time for grandchildren. How I longed for them ... Maybe if I'd had those other children. You know they say that abortion can raise your risk of cancer, and I had two. One before Shae and another one after. Then I had my tubes tied, but I regret it. I regretted it a year later once I truly knew I wasn't going to conceive again."

"Why did you?"

"What? End the pregnancies? Sometimes I wonder. I was sick, so sick I couldn't stand it and found myself almost praying, 'Please let this be over, let me have a miscarriage.' Then I thought why can't I? I'd actually marched for reproductive rights. So I did."

"But you had Shae."

"I felt just a little sick with Shae. They say that one gender or the other will make the mother sicker. Maybe they were girls. I hate to think that now. I would have loved to have daughters. Then I wanted grandchildren so badly. I didn't really care how they came. I just wanted them."

I'm quiet, wondering if I'm hearing what she means for me to hear.

"I was so heartbroken when you stopped coming here. Shae never told me why, but I want you to know, I wouldn't have minded, not one bit, if you and Shae had gotten pregnant."

"That would have been a disaster for me," I say and smile, reminding her that she can't be serious.

"We delay things too long in this culture. You were a mature girl, a smart girl. Sometimes having too much choice about these things just takes what we want away from us."

I don't look at her and she flutters a little beside me, presses my arm gently with her dry palm.

"But that's all idle speculation, isn't it? You have a rich life, an important life."

She takes out another photo album, leaving the old one open on the coffee table.

"And here's my sweetie, Erica, Shae's daughter. I went over to Lagos for the birth."

I'm looking at a photo of Janine holding the tightly bundled newborn, and although I can't really see her face clearly, I tell her that the baby is beautiful.

"But when she was born I told myself I better not get too attached. I could see the marriage wasn't working out. His wife is ... tight, too tight for him."

I could mistake her intention, so discombobulated I am by the direction this whole conversation has taken. Is she too tight for him sexually, is this what Janine is saying? What exactly does she mean? She reads my mind again and laughs, saying again, "I mean wound tight like a spring. Tense."

She tells me she only saw her grandchild that once, three years ago when she was there for the birth. Being there, actually helping in the room, was a miracle. Shae came home to arrange for her to get some help when she first started chemotherapy but Karen and the baby stayed in Africa. She hasn't been well enough or free enough from treatment to fly halfway around the world.

She flips to the earlier pages of the album, settling on a two-page spread that is so intimate I at first look away.

Karen, Shae's wife, is lying on her side in obvious pain, one hand grasping the railing of the hospital bed. Then she's propped up on her back with her eyes closed. Her hospital gown is lifted and Shae's hands are on her belly. I purposely don't look at the patch of hair between her legs. The photo on the next page gives me no choice: it's a close up of her pubis, the baby's darker hair just visible beyond the purplish bulge, the extended lips. I hope Janine was using a zoom and not perched on the bed leaning in for the shot. Then a photo of Karen pushing, being held up by Shae. Her delicate face from earlier photographs is unrecognizable. She's snarling, mouth open, all the power of her neck, arms, legs focused on this one task. Then blood in the bed, the spiraling tough purple cord as the baby is held above her, but still tethered to her mother's body. The stitching, the exhaustion, the baby put to her mother's breast. I see a smear of blood near Karen's armpit, her nipple pulled like taffy. In the next photo, Shae holds his wife's breast to the baby's mouth.

Janine notices me shifting away from the album. It's too intimate, studying this woman at her most vulnerable.

"I'm sorry, Marylee. I've been insensitive. That's what you most want yourself, a baby. I shouldn't have shown you these photos."

We talk more about my parents, whom she is glad to hear are well. She tells me about some of the teachers at the high school who've died. I pour another cup of tea from the pottery teapot so that I don't seem to be in too much of a hurry, but I manage to finish off the cup in a couple of minutes because the tea has cooled. I rise to leave. As she's lifting my coat off the hanger in the front hall, she says, "You should come back in a couple of weeks. Shae will be here for meetings at the end of January. You two could catch up."

"That would be nice," I tell her. She hugs me, hard, and I feel the ribs in her back, strangely close to her spine. I hold her an extra minute to transfer my warmth to her because I know I'll never see her again.

Lucky

A FEW MONTHS BEFORE MY FATHER DIED, he won over $95,000 at the casino across the river, not all at once, but over a couple of weeks, in the middle of the night when I thought he was sleeping. It was like the blast of light before a star burns out—that last run of spectacular luck.

"Why didn't you call me when the furnace died?" I asked him.

The cold had awakened him and he dressed, fetched his fanny pack of poker chips and money from his hiding place in the basement and called a taxi to take him to a place he knew was warm and welcoming 24 hours a day. I could imagine him at three in the morning standing in his black leather jacket, plaid scarf, and matching leather newsboy cap at the dining room window watching for the sweep of headlights across the dry snow, the heft of the black car lifting little whirlpools of tiny sequins as the taxi pulled up the driveway. Then, leaning against an icy middle-of-the-night blackness, my father would have had to steady himself with his hand on the warm hood, heard the ticking of the warm motor, then smelled the air-freshened chemical scent of pine.

"It was Valentine's Day. I didn't want to take you away from your sweetie. And maybe you'd had a little too much to drink."

"You could have taken the taxi to my place. I wouldn't leave you out in the cold," I said but he didn't answer because this hasn't always been true. When he was drinking and out of control I did leave him out in the cold, for years in fact. Left out on my doorstep, banging on the glass to be acknowledged, out of my life for as long as I could stand the guilt. This current period of diligent closeness was so unexpected, maybe he didn't trust it. Being the good daughter was certainly a strange experience for me. Being back in his life when he was 84 years old meant that I'd be there for the long haul, whatever that would mean. I knew that, but maybe he didn't. I must have seemed as ephemeral and unreliable as he had been when I was growing up.

"Good thing I didn't," he said. "I wouldn't have anything to show for lying in bed like an old man. You've got to get out there and strike when the iron's hot. That's what I told the guy who drove me home."

"You shouldn't have told him you'd won. How much money did you have?"

"About $40,000."

"You told a taxi driver that you had that kind of cash on you?" I was so alarmed I was almost yelling at him, but my father just laughed.

"The guy said, 'In my dreams. I'm that lucky in my dreams.'"

"He could have mugged you! Thrown you into a ditch. He could have helped you into the house and pushed you down the stairs."

"Not Fariq. He said to call him any time. Gave me his personal number."

He must have used that personal number a few more times because by the end of February he claimed to be close to $100,000.

"It's your mother," he said when I drove him to the bank, insisting that he deposit all but a few hundred of the money he won at the casino. But he kept thousands of dollars in his back pocket. Maybe more—even in old age he had the habits of an addict. Would his luck go this way or that? Either way, he would hedge his bets. Make sure he could keep going. Even though he was letting me take him to the bank, he had his plans. I could tell by the way he was looking at his fingernails and not at me, his wrists turned towards his body as though he was already holding a hand of cards, protective and secretive, as if sheltering something that could fly up out of his grasp.

"I found her little purse. The one she wore over her shoulder, all packed and ready to go, with lucky chips, lipstick and 200 dollars in coins. You know how she liked the slots. No skill in that, the odds are all for the house, but she enjoyed it. Now she's my lucky charm."

My mother had died the fall before, leaving him alone in the big suburban house with too much garden to tend. This was the last thing I would have expected. He had always been the one suddenly in intensive care after another suicide attempt, four in all. But he was lucky a student noticed the light on in his office one Sunday night. Lucky the neighbor heard his car running in the garage another time. Lucky he didn't have brain damage. Lucky liver, lucky kidneys. Lucky the police didn't stop him when he lightly bounced off the abutment, that he never had a car accident, killed a child, lost his job.

Thinking of these dark possible outcomes that he'd somehow dodged, I felt the same wave of shame I felt years ago when I dropped by a party at the university celebrating his 20 years as a professor. From the doorway of the darkened room, I saw him in his old Air Force uniform doing a crazy dance punctuated by deep bends from the waist that showed off his blazingly white underwear because the too-tight pants had split. Whoo! The crowd went wild every time he took that dip, usually off-time to the loud rock music. As far as I could tell, the room was filled with students and not his colleagues. My mother hadn't gone to the party—she never did—and he had wanted at least part of his family there.

I left to wait for him by the front doors. That was February too and the streets were thick with black serpent-patterned slush, a hissing as cars passed. Eventually the party sounds started to die down, so I went back in, took his keys from his jacket pocket, put him in the back seat of his own Cutlass Supreme and drove him home as he, still in high spirits, sang "MacNamara's Band" out of tune. My mother hadn't waited up.

Now that he was sober, he liked to take taxis everywhere, as though he didn't need to prove any more how lucky he was. His mood swings had moderated with old age so that I was taken off guard by this surge of energy in the middle of the night. My mother had never seemed particularly surprised by what her life with him threw at her. With her firm resolve, she kept to her schedule of giving piano lessons in the afternoons, watching Jeopardy in the evenings, deadheading roses in the summer. The Sunday morning she was told by the resident doctor that the leukemia diagnosed the week before would take her life was the day she willfully fell asleep and slipped away without a goodbye. She hadn't won much at slots, but she had won the death lottery.

"I feel badly that she didn't get to go again. She was packed and ready, but we didn't go and then she died."

This sad little narrative is a lot less complicated than their marriage was.

"So take me, Dad. I'll go with you."

He clucked, half laugh, half reprimand, and I could hear his dentures click. He had lost weight since my mother died and nothing seemed to fit him right. We were still sitting in the bank's parking lot steaming up the windows.

"There's no need for that. You never liked games. Not even cards when you were little."

"You're right. I always felt trapped, like I was waiting for Godot."

"Who?" my father said.

"Godot. It's a play. The coin falls the same way every time, with no way out."

"If that's the way life worked out, you'd win every time. If you knew ... "

"But that's it, Dad. You don't know. You're just stuck in the pattern and have no real control."

He shrugged and looked out at the parking lot. We had reached an impasse of sorts. He was hoarding his optimism, keeping it away from my dark fatalism. But I couldn't let it go. For some reason, he made me angry.

"I'm not that lucky, you know," I said.

"You're alive, aren't you?" he said but his voice was pensive, not snappish at all and I felt a little ashamed of my words, as though I was whining.

"Yes, you're right. It's a billion-to-one shot that I'm even here. Me and my broken cookie jar."

"What cookie jar?" he asked.

"The only thing I ever won was a Noah's ark cookie jar made in China. The giraffe snapped off at the neck within a couple of weeks. I won it at a bridal shower for a wedding that never happened."

"Why not?"

"The bride-to-be slashed her fiancé's leather couch with a knife and drove away—recklessly—into the night."

He laughed. "He must have made her awfully mad."

"Drinking was involved."

"Well, those are some little kids that will never get born. And maybe that's the biggest stroke of luck of all."

I was surprised at this conversation, how perceptive, how direct, and so unlike the father I had known, who seemed so oblivious to life and so uneasy in his own skin most of the time, or at least when he was sober. Now that he was alone and in his eighties, he was taking a clear-eyed look around.

THIS IS HOW I end up at the casino with my father. He's dressed in his best Las Vegas style, with a turquoise-stone cowboy tie cinched in with narrow leather cords, white shoes and a charcoal dress jacket that sharpens his shoulders and emits a faint sheen, almost electrical, like the skin of something that lives underwater in the dark. He sits below me at the high rollers' blackjack table and I can smell his strong aftershave, a little too assertive, and the whiff of his urine bag strapped to his thigh. I'm used to it when he's at home, but here, the smell is unpleasant and I wonder if the pretty woman standing before him dealing cards is holding her breath.

I am standing too, behind him, just to his right, and I wonder if he senses me, but he seems completely engaged in the game. Something brings out a side of him I have never seen before. He's not grunting, caveman style, but he might as well be with the abrupt and bossy way he uses his hands. He taps his index finger on the green felt table to indicate that he wants a card, flicks the same finger dismissively, as though shaking off gristle and fat while dressing down a deer, when he's decided to hold. The dealer follows his cues with her eyes. The exchange between them is wordless. And chips change hands. He loses $500, then gains $800. Neither of them acknowledges the loss or gain. She rakes his chips towards her firm belly or pushes them towards him. Her motions are like a tide sweeping a beach clean.

Then he's down $5,000 and produces a handful of $1,000 chips from his inside breast coat pocket.

"Dad," I whisper, "Didn't you have a limit? You didn't buy those tonight." He closes his hands over the chips and leans his knuckles into his chest where his heart is so that I understand that these are the lucky chips that he's carried with him from the night he found my mother's purse. He's spending his luck, like seed potatoes that have already yielded so much.

Although he seems in control, I see that one of his pants pockets is inside out, a flash of white like the tail of a fleeing deer. A dark bird flies across the overhead lights, but when I look up there's nothing there. I think of that old saying: *We enter and leave life with no pockets.*

The dealer doesn't look above my father's bald head. My hope to catch her sympathetic eye fades although I don't know what I mean to accomplish with my worried expression, my lifted brows. The cold at my back shifts as I'm aware of the warm presence of other people suddenly drawn to this table. All around me are other silent standing witnesses, barely breathing as he throws himself upon the laws of chance. Others are drawn to witness spectacular losses and gains. The hum of the slot machines beyond this quiet room is a constant high-pitched whirr of music, tuning for an orchestra that never begins, a spaceship that never lands, an expectation, anticipation, a sound calibrated to heighten the nervous system to alertness, a wind keening, carrying all of us towards the end of the world.

I can't stand to watch my father any more. What bothers me is not really the throwing away of money, thousands at a time, but the prurient crowd pressing close to him that risks nothing.

"I'll be in the slots room," I tell him, but he's too focused to do more than nod.

I find a quiet row and fish some quarters out of my purse but can't find a place to insert them into the machine. The directions are too small to read without my glasses so I sit staring at the little cartoon cherry, watermelon, two oranges that spell out the last gambler's parting shot.

"You need to put money on a card," the man seated beside me says, not turning to look at me, not breaking his rhythm on the slot machine. "Machines don't take change any more."

"Thanks. Do you mind if I just watch?"

His focus and the way he nods reminds me of my father, although this man looks as though he's been down on his luck all his life. We're sitting off in this row of machines away from the crowds. These are the five-cent machines, unattractive to the glitzy gamblers in evening wear and high heels.

The sleeves of his plaid shirt are rolled up to his elbows, his jeans are cinched in by a leather belt and there are deep furrows on his brow and beside his mouth. His lips move slightly and I imagine a sibilant whispering sound although I can't hear over the loud hum and ringing of the machines.

He hits the button with his closed fist and swiftly opens his hands, palms to the glass, to cover the spinning symbols. He only removes his hands when the line is fixed. Then again and again, in perfect rhythm, he hits and hides, hits and hides.

"Is that part of the game?" I ask him. "Are you more likely to win that way?"

"It's just superstition," he says.

If he can't see what is coming, maybe the gods are more likely to be generous. If he is humble and patient and waits, even when the nights are so long they seem to go on forever.

I WAS LUCKY those afternoons after winter had retreated from the yard, the way time slowed down to sleeping and waking, occasional words.

More than most people, he must have known from an early age that death obliterates the numbers, or at least fixes them so that they have no vitality any more. Near the end, when he was weak but still came downstairs to sit in his easy chair in the sun, he told me that his grandfather had been a stonemason and had carved his own tombstone, along with his daughter's and my grandfather's. The stones were stored in the seed shed, too heavy to shift, but my father saw them from early childhood with their patient dates carved into the stone, grey granite for the men, pink for his mother, chiseled with the years of their births and the expectant hyphen.

"The stones vanished, one at a time," he said sadly. "First my grandfather's, then my father's. When they reappeared in the grave-yard with those end dates carved as though by the very same hand, it was as shocking to me as the mysteries of Easter Island."

"Or Stonehenge," I said.

"Lost people. Just gone."

I could feel him tallying up numbers, seeing again those grave-stones facing the sea in Nova Scotia. His grandfather—88 years; his father—83 years; and his mother—93 years.

What did your dad die of?" I asked him.

"Oh, just old age," he answered, as though this state of affairs had nothing to do with him.

After a pause, he told me, "If I only got two more years from treatment, it wouldn't be worth it. But I'm fine here. I'm content." He must have done the calculations and estimated that he should be good for 89 years, far more than the 84 he currently had.

Less than two months is what he had from that moment of calculation.

WHAT WAS LEFT of the money he won, after a month-long losing streak, was spent on private nursing care, even when I had to be home or at work, so that he was never alone and no matter what he would never be subjected to the cheap exhibit of a flashing red light on the quiet crescent, no noisy sirens hospital-bound. No more being ferried across the river to open himself to fate. Fate was right there, in his dim bed-room where the curtains were drawn against the strong summer light.

He stopped drinking ginger ale one morning. Swallowing must have taken enormous energy because for the last couple of days he'd left his lids half-closed, his eyes rolled slightly upwards as though he was seeing a flickering reflection on the inside of his forehead.

I put the glass with its straw down and held his gaze.

"All done, then?" I asked.

He didn't nod, but he closed his eyes. All that was left was the waiting. I didn't long for the waiting to be over. His breathing changed like waves, shallower, then deeper, shallower and deeper, absences of breath now and then before the tentative intake of air started again. He needed nothing from me. I didn't need to be there, but I wanted to be. How fortunate for me that our relationship would end when my orbit had swung back from the cold of deep space. In my years of being apart from him, I imagined how I would receive news of his death. I had steeled myself to distance, the protection of a starless void between us, expecting that he would die one day by his own hand.

During the last day or so, I sat staring at the dim white wall of his bedroom, not at him, wanting to give him some privacy and dignity. Memories of our past formed, vague and blurry, as though the wall was hung with an old sheet like those Sixties slideshows I only ever saw at other people's houses. The images were fewer in number than I would have thought. The last six months were the most vivid. I thought of the morning, just six weeks before, when he was told that tumours lined his liver and lungs, his nodes, his viscera, and he asked me, "If it came on this fast, do you think it could disappear just as fast?"

"I don't really think so," I say. "No. Probably not."

He was a living but finite man and maybe he deserved to hear better odds. I wish that I'd gone along with his hopes, given him a few more imagined years. Those years he felt entitled to now that there was peace after grief, his daughter back in his life, a run of good fortune. I wish I'd been more generous. Maybe he was asking for my words, my own hopes for him to be in my life longer. He wanted me to fill with ardent beliefs the way his wallet and pockets filled up with chips and cash, the way his body filled with the sinister exuberance of his own cells.

Feigning Death

I'VE FINALLY STARTED DREAMING about my mother. In the first dream she was quiet, buried under the driveway asphalt. Then I met her on the street—a polite greeting between the two of us. Finally, she's sitting with me in my house, dividing up her possessions although there is no one else there to take what they are owed.

"I could give you the silver tea set," she offers and I consider and decline. Her hostility is not aroused so I know this is a dream.

"But I'd like the tea cups from your bridal shower," I say and she agrees, evenly. She picks up a blue-flowered cup and saucer that have miraculously appeared between us and they change hands.

Then she lifts the next object from my cherry table suddenly laden with these objects from my childhood. She holds her opal ring that is surprisingly not on her finger, as though considering where it best belongs. Her death is not mentioned or grieved although this is understood as the reason for this meeting.

"It's beautiful," I say quietly and she nods a little sadly, very regal, her hair blue-black as the last queen of Ireland she claimed she was descended from.

Then she puts the ring down between us without offering it to me. Her fingers are long and strong, the good architecture of a pianist.

THIS DREAM WAS so different from the last interaction I had with my mother in real life. A couple of hours before she died she rose from her bed and put her hands around my throat, softly reaching all the way around to the back of my neck—those strong dry fingers slipping into position with all her strength held in abeyance. The sensation was much like that of a milk snake that was once draped over my shoulders, the slide of its languid dry weight around my bare neck. Her hands felt as strong as that, and leisurely, as though there was all the time in the world.

I rose up gasping from the reclined chair, my heart pounding, an awkward scramble that seems to have become part of my physical vocabulary since turning 50. The light from the streets outside the hospital flickered across her bed. She hadn't moved. The bruised arm lay still along her side, her face was angled slightly away from me. My hand was still holding the ball of her foot pointed as though wearing invisible high heels. Her stillness was a trick she was playing on me, as though feigning death.

WITHIN A FEW DAYS of her death, my brother and I started to tear her drawers and closets apart, pitching concert programs that dated back to the 1940s. *Look* magazines from the 1960s, olive-green sweaters pilled and stretched, pointy-toed shoes, crushed hats with moth-eaten fishnet veils and feathers, lists of her piano students and a tally of the fees they paid, starting with $2.00 just after the war, rising precipitously through the prosperity of the 1970s and reaching her all-time high of $40.00 an hour. We didn't have the fortitude to call back the last student she had when she went into the hospital, an innocent voice on the answering machine wondering about her next lesson. Lists and expenses and receipts. My face grew hot when I saw newspaper clippings about my books, my younger face pixelated and yellowed. Little had I known all that she recorded, how much she needed to hang on to.

When my brother was out of the room, I opened her secret drawer, stuffed full of stockings with seams up the backs, holy cards of the Virgin Mary dated each Christmas in her own mother's hand in dark blue fountain pen, a couple of rosaries with tiny black prayer beads, and a surprising number of little leather-bound prayer books. I lifted a Crown Royal bag heavy and shifting with old costume jewelry, rifled through the treasures that I hadn't been allowed to take away when I was a child. I emptied her good purse, feeling a little sick, seeing all her things useless and unneeded. So I filled it with my own wallet and hairbrush.

I took her lipsticks from the ledge in her bathroom so my father wouldn't have to see them lined up there, all dark shades. I felt like I was thieving and couldn't bear to slide the plum colour onto my lips. It smelled a little off, like meat covered over by a flowery chemical scent.

SHE HOLDS OUT her closed hand, looking at me with some impatience. Her diamond wedding ring flashes, prismatic. I cup my hand below her fist and wonder what she will let fall. Sand or dust or tiny bones. But a slippery shape falls almost weightless onto my palm. A salamander, skin as tender and dark as a bruise. A tickle, a whisper of movement and it's gone.

WE STOPPED AT THE THRESHOLD, became invisible under our pale gowns, our gloves cooling our hands, masks locking in our breath so that our voices echoed in our heads. Only she was flesh and breath and vivid with life, the bag of scarlet seeming to run out of her veins instead of the other way around. Five years is a long time. She looked at my grown children and at me. "Your eyes are the same," she said. Something essential recognized, finally. But my daughter interpreted it differently. "That's genetics. They're probably the same as yours." She seemed detached but not at all unhappy that we were there.

"No appetite," she said. I threaded a straw through the hole in her oxygen mask misted with her heat and she drank quietly, the spirit level rising ever so slightly, the lightness of her need like the feet of water gliders on a side pool as the stream tumbled over rocks and fallen logs, obstacles of life, just one channel over. One day later, her last word in answer to my question, "You seem to be in pain? Do you want anything?" "No," the final word, whispered, with a drawing-in of her eyebrows, too tired to open her eyes. All the rest was dreams and mystery.

SOMETHING RATTLES IN her pocket like keys, but she pulls out a heavy rusty link of chain that was once attached to a crane, some monolithic machine that moved earth. I remember the chain but haven't thought about it in decades. I found it in a construction site where we weren't allowed to play. Imitating the saints, instead of a scapula, I wore it under my uniform. And then it became a compulsion and I was never free of it—this heavy rusty link on a scratchy piece of twine, bruising my tender chest, the smell of iron rising from my clothes when I sat at school, head down, doing my work.

"You think I don't know what is under your clothes? And it makes such a mess of the sheets. Rust on white cotton can leave a permanent stain. I scrub and scrub."

"So you did take it away. One morning it was just gone."

"Yes, I did," she says, challenging me. "What a strange child you are."

"You should talk," I say. "What's with all those holy cards and prayer books in your secret drawer? I never hear you refer to religion."

She waves her hand dismissively. "Those are for my mother. She needed to give them to me so she could rest in peace. What can I do? Throw them away?"

FORCED AND UNCOORDINATED, her body persevered. The chest rose jagged, the soul dragged behind this cranky machine. Hard, painful work that cannot be refused. The gowns and masks were discarded. We were nakedly ourselves because we could not hurt her any more.

"You should write more comic stories," my sister told me as our mother slept. She was so pallid and glassy-eyed herself, she could have been the one in the bed. When she entered the room and put her bicycle seat and helmet down on the spare chair, a strange smell of sweat and desperation spread like damp spores over our mother's clean sheets. I wanted to sweep it off my shoulders.

"Why should I?"

"You could be funny if you wanted to be."

"But funny wouldn't be worth the hard work. Writing is really hard work. I guess I'm in it for something else."

"But there's no resolution in your stories. Great composers always resolve the tension in their work. Mozart..."

"Mozart is over. Long gone."

But our mother was still dying and nothing was resolved. Her chest resisted breath and her abdomen, made of softer stuff, rose spasmodically. There was a little huff at the end of each exhalation. We glanced across the bed, at a loss at how to move from this point onwards. The hospital curtain drifted against my neck and I shivered.

"A short story is not a novel. A poem is not a short story. The forms are different."

" Isn't that convenient. It's over when you say it's over, right?"

My mother could not rise and walk out of the room as she did when any conflict was imminent. I said it for her, just once, for my mother who was angered by what I created.

"Literature that I care about reveals what's hidden and leaves it luminous or illuminated, not resolved. Maybe I don't believe that tensions resolve."

Our mother did not break us up, send us to our rooms. She did not turn towards one side or another. Suddenly, I felt more solid in the chair. I could breathe a little easier. My sister must have noticed this.

"Don't you feel guilty being here, after five years? Mom just wanted privacy—the one thing you couldn't give. She didn't want her life used like that, for fodder."

"Music is easier, I know. It skips the gossip."

MY MOTHER REACHES behind her, shifting heavily on my uncomfortable wooden chair. Her arm is straining. She's wearing her pale lilac dress with the permanent crinkles that stretch to smoothness over her right breast, and three strands of plum-coloured artificial pearls. She places the purple Crown Royal bag on the table between us.

"This is your chance," she says. "No more playing dress-up. Now you take my jewelry for good." She laughs. When I don't answer, she says, "Yes? Or no?"

The bag is rolling a little on the table, churning with something caught inside. I'm afraid to touch it.

"Go on," she urges. So I lay my hand on the soft flannel and suddenly the bag is quiet and inert. I loosen the gold silky rope, the tassels tickling the tops of my hands, the sensation of a fly bothering the surface of my skin, but I don't sweep it away.

My hand slips into the bag, which is moist, warm and muscular, tunnelling tighter, constricting my hand, almost crushing my fingers. Yet, I know to push further.

When I withdraw my glistening hand, I'm holding a painted egg, weightless.

"It's beautiful," I gasp.

She smiles, maybe a little smug. "I painted it myself. With hot wax, and dipped it in dye baths, blue after green, after blue, then black."

"I didn't know you could do this!"

"There are plenty of things you don't know about me."

The egg lies on its side in my hand, the top half a stormy slate blue, the bottom half a rough ocean of sea-green, turquoise and black waves. Around the circumference are three leaning ships, their billowing white sails the only place where the colour of the egg is unadulterated.

"Nina, Pinta and the Santa Maria," she says. "You know your brother is getting the piano, and your sister will take all the albums and CDs, but this is for you."

"Thank you so much! I'll treasure it. I'll keep it safe." I turn the egg to examine the south and the north poles. The axes are tiny pinpricks where the liquids were blown out.

LET HER DREAM, I told the cough that roused her. Let her be, as I removed her mask and put the tissue to her mouth where it blossomed dark red like her favourite roses. I dipped a swab in clear water and cleaned her mouth, a whisper of water and soft pink foam. Her face mottled then, a blueness spread around the mouth and eyes. When I put the mask back on, the blue retreated, letting us know it was waiting and patient.

"You almost killed Mom," my brother said, meeting my eye. We both looked away and quietly laughed.

SHE LIFTS THE LID on her sewing box. It's angled so that I can see the pins stuck into the swollen red cushion of its silk lining. Sharp silver needles without heads, frozen sleet. The tin of buttons rattles but what she lifts from the box, one by one, are pill bottles. She places them between us, some squat and glass, others tall with tinted orange plastic and childproof lids.

"You're old enough to open these yourself," she says. "I don't have to worry about you any more, finally!"

I read the bottles: coated aspirin for her arthritis, antihistamines for allergies, oxycontin for pain.

"But I have no pain."

"Yes, you do," she says, sizing me up.

THE NURSE'S SKIN was black and glistening as though it wasn't November in the northern hemisphere. Water was not enough, so he swabbed her mouth with white cream, the oxygen mask on the pillow beside her.

"Last Friday, she told me about her son, the musician. And she talked about her daughter, "the spy". She was so proud of her daughter." He smiled at me.

"That's my sister. She's a mathematician and a decoder."

He looked at me quizzically, holding the swab in his broad warm hand. I could see that he had no idea then who I was.

"I'm the writer. She wasn't particularly proud of me."

"Stop talking to him," my sister said. "Stop distracting him. I want that mask back on."

"He knows his job. He wouldn't harm her."

"I want that mask back on right now."

MY MOTHER PLACES a blue construction paper Mother's Day card on the table between us. The flower on the cover is three-dimensional, made with crushed little pieces of red tissue paper, glued in the shape of a sunburst flower with a black crayon heart. I remember the smell of the glue, its crusty snuffling pig's nose pressing flat against the paper and the way the tissue paper stuck to my fingers, staining them bright red. I peeled a thin layer of red off my hands as though removing my own fingerprints. Only the flower stands stiff and upright—the stem is flat green and waxy crayon. The card will not lie closed on the table. I pick it up and it falls open in my hand. I read out loud, having no inkling of ever having written the contents.

Children's Need

I know you have to get mad at me,
But if you didn't I don't know what I'd be.
But then again if I didn't have you,
I just don't know what I would do.

My voice quavers a little by the last line. My mother smiles at me a little triumphantly. "Oh, it isn't as bad as all that," she says.

I laugh. I'm starting to catch on to her little jokes, double entendres, this new directness.

"Oh, but it is horrible poetry. I *do* you so much better in the writing you refuse to read."

"Yes, I'm 'done' all right. All done up and nowhere to go. My mother will be so disappointed when I don't arrive."

SLEEPING, OUR BREATHS were a disjointed syncopation. Go to her, resist, go to her, resist, and I slid into wakefulness when the nurse stood at the curtain to listen to my mother's breathing. Gentler breathing, like waves at night, one wave in seven so soft, there was silence. The nurse's white shape withdrew and the light from the door narrowed to a slit. She breathed and then she stopped. I held my breath and waited and she did not resume although I had to, after a slow exhalation. I stood beside her bed. Her eyes were closed, the mask empty as a shell that I lifted from the sand, and I heard a soft roar in my head.

"YOU WERE BORN too sensitive," my mother says. She's not holding anything for me, but maybe this admission is the gift.

"Or maybe allergic to me. You came out mottled and red, screaming, covered with a rash."

"Maybe you were the one allergic," I say. "Allergic to me inside you." My heart beats fast, expecting her wrath, but she only shrugs.

"Either way, you looked like a burn victim. I thought, this poor child, going through life with skin like that. All inflamed and sensitive."

"It went away."

"Not completely. When you cry I can see the red marks. A horseshoe of red between your eyes. Of course, I haven't seen you cry in years."

"I cry. Believe me, I cry."

LIQUID SOAP, green as spring and her fingers slipped between my hands but the rings could not move past the arthritic joint. So later that night, when it finally happened, she would go to the morgue wearing only her wedding rings. And the next day, the rings delivered to me from the undertaker in a sealed envelope that I tore open like a looter, intact, not cut where the gold was thinnest. What had to be severed to give these to me so unflawed?

"We're not going there," my brother said. All the strength of her hands released now, the staccato left hand cut free from the pattern, the passion of her alone in a room, thunderous throughout the house.

§

SHE PICKS UP THE OPAL RING that has been sitting between us, ignored all this time. She tries to slip it on her own finger, but it can't pass the arthritic joint.

"Don't hurt yourself," I say and she laughs.

"A little late for that!"

"All I mean is don't force it."

"You're right. I don't need it now. " She places it on her palm, empty of lines, and reaches across the table. The ring tumbles from her hand and falls into mine.

"Give it to your daughter."

"Your granddaughter." I insist.

"Yes, my grandchild. Her memories are few and far between but this is something."

I STAYED THE COURSE, the dim lights elongating as they swept along her inert shape, relieved finally to be alone with her, her cooling foot in my hand. The tranquilizer I'd taken in the bathroom dissolved time. There was the sound of drills in the floors above, construction until past midnight. Light and shadow, light and shadow, and remembered the construction too on the hospital where I gave birth to my daughter. Alone at night, throbbing from the rent in my belly. Unable to shake the sensation of a man's hands inside me, pulling life from the split pod. Daughter arriving, mother leaving, the same.

And again, she seemed to rise as I dozed, leaning over me and slipping her hands softly around my throat, gently, but with the press of need. As though insisting another time because I missed it the first time, *notice me, notice me.*

She was blessing your voice.
That was her parting shot.
Just a hallucination caused by being overtired and stressed.

There was no other place you would rather be.
Five years of absence made this last moment the only moment possible.
Your last challenge before the relationship is fixed and static and finished.
You brought her no comfort and should have left.
Nothing else mattered; she wanted to touch you purely, without language.
Why did you need to create this image for yourself?
A mother's hands speak of the needs she can't express verbally.
Her desire to hang onto you …
Her desire to hang you …
Her desire …

THE SKY BEYOND the window lightens to November grey. It's the first dawn she isn't here. She and I are both tired from the long night of the hard labour of dying. She stirs in her bed, lifts arms that lost all strength days ago and admires their cool long length. She turns her palm over, opens her fingers and offers me her silver lipstick. I take it, twist the base, bend towards her as though to whisper in her ear. But instead, I reach out and gently glide the colour over her lips and the dark plum turns blue when it touches her skin. She smiles at me with her vivid cold mouth, and unafraid then, I kiss her.

Acknowledgements:

The following stories have appeared in publication previously: "The Story of Time" (*Prairie Fire*), "Heart of Blue, Glowing" (*Prairie Fire*), "Blood Secrets" (*Prairie Fire*), "Where All the Ladders Start" (*The New Quarterly*), "Bare Bones" (*Decalogue: Ten Ottawa Fiction Writers*), "Persephone Without Maps" (*Prism International*) and "Lucky" (*Best Canadian Stories: 2012*).

The author would like to acknowledge the Ontario Arts Council, the City of Ottawa and The Banff Centre for financial assistance that allowed her to complete this book.

About the Author

Nadine McInnis is the author of seven books, the most recent being *Two Hemispheres* (Brick Books, Fall 2007), a book-length poetic exploration of illness and health partially inspired by the first medical photographs of women patients of the Surrey County Lunatic Asylum in 1850, which was shortlisted for the 2008 Pat Lowther Award, the ReLit Award, the People's Choice Award and the Lampman-Scott Award. Her other books include *First Fire / ce feu qui devore*, a bilingual selected and new poems, *Quicksilver* (short fiction), *Hand to Hand* (poetry); *Poetics of Desire*, a critical study of the love poems of Dorothy Livesay, *The Litmus Body* (poetry) and *Shaking the Dreamland Tree* (poetry). Her last collection of short stories, *Quicksilver,* was shortlisted for the Danuta Gleed Award for best first book of short stories by a Canadian, The Writers Craft Award for best book of short stories by an Ontario author and the Ottawa Book Award. She's also a past prizewinner in the CBC Literary Competition. She is currently coordinator of the Professional Writing Program at Algonquin College.